Conflict
Rise Of Mankind Book 4

John Walker

Copyright © 2016 John Walker

DISCLAIMER

This is a work of fiction. Names, characters, business, places, events, and incidents are either the products of the author's imagination or used in a fictitious manner. Any resemblance to actual persons, living or dead, or actual events is purely coincidental. This story contains explicit language and violence.

Blurb

Disaster strikes

The Behemoth, en route home after a successful mission liberating a mining facility from pirates, finds itself drifting in an uncharted sector of space. As the crew comes to, made ill by this jump drive malfunction, they spring into action to restore the ship to operational status so they can get home.

However, they quickly find they are not alone. Surrounded by a native fleet of warships, they are viewed with suspicion as an alien force infringing on another culture's space. They attempt to communicate but find themselves moving toward a conflict they do not want. The Behemoth may find themselves stuck in the far reaches of space with no hope of getting home.

Prologue

An explosion off the port bow drew Raeka's attention to the main screen. One of his destroyers took a direct hit to the engine room, obliterating the reactor and sending two hundred men and women to their deaths. Ordinance of all types flew in every direction, decorating the empty space with streaks of red and purple.

Two fleets engaged in an epic struggle. The Emancipated versus Founders. As they pressed hard for any advantage, smaller vessels burned and popped in orange ovals before flickering out of existence like a candle snuffed by the fingers of a God. The upper hand seemed elusive and the fight might've gone on for several hours.

Raeka Anvinari commanded the Emancipated fleet, sending commands to the various ships as they countered the even odds of their enemies. Scout vessels attempted to flank their adversaries, launching missiles before using superior speed to dart away, out of range. Turrets from battleships lobbed heavy projectiles against the shields of the larger capital ships but hadn't been able to break through.

All this death, all this conflict. How can our leaders not find a common ground to build a lasting peace? Raeka had long been weary of fighting. All the young soldiers under his command who died needlessly deserved better. Instead, the politicians played dangerous games and created nothing but tension and new grudges.

The captain stood tall for one of his kind at just over six feet and his slate black hair was cut short in the tradition of a warrior. Brown-black eyes peered out from a severe brow and his figure, thin and tone, wore his uniform easily, as if he were born to it. As he leaned forward, chin on his hand, he peripherally realized he needed to shave—just a slight distraction to his wholly focused attention.

Much as he wanted to practice what he thought, Raeka believed the Founders were little more than spoiled bullies, trying to steal what they didn't earn. Sharing might've been possible if they had been willing to be something other than tyrants. As soon as they began to *demand* and even tried to *steal* the hard work of the colonists, the fighting started.

It all started long before Raeka was born and he grew up in a world obsessed with the conflict. Everyone discussed it as if there were no other topics. Social concerns fell by the wayside and as he ordered another volley of missiles to be thrown against their enemies, he wondered if there ever might come a day where they worked together again.

"Direct hit!" Tarkin, the weapon's officer cried. "We missed their flagship but one of the picket line vessels just went down."

"Very good," Raeka replied. "Let's get into a better position to finish this off. It would be nice to enjoy a decisive victory today."

He stood by and watched as their ships took advantage of the breach in the enemy's line. They sent a massive barrage against the Founder flagship, watching as the shields flared wildly from so many hits. Still, they managed to hold and Tarkin cursed under his breath, reorganizing his people for another attack.

Before they'd be ready, the Founder commander would certainly close the gap. Those front line ships projected a dome like shield, granting protection to all the vessels behind them as well. These single direction barriers allowed them to fire out but kept anything from getting through.

They had to overwhelm the one ship they took out in order to blow it up. Their scouts could help but they didn't carry heavy enough weapons to do *too* much damage. This meant they needed to throw even more ordinance out but luckily, they didn't have to worry much about ammunition.

Their mass driving cannons could recreate additional rounds from scrap and they carried an awful lot when engaging in fleet actions. Beam weapons were less reliable but they did help once they burst through shields. They could cut sections of enemy ships off quite easily but did not allow for sustained weapon use.

Each blast tended to sap their reserve of energy and required them to recharge. Depending on how overboard they went with using them, that could last five minutes or extend to several hours. Raeka had ordered such an attack once that debilitated their ship for nearly a day but it had been a decisive win against an enemy ship depot.

It set the Founders back six months on replacing lost ships so the price was more than worth paying.

Raeka watched as the Founders moved into a formation he was quite familiar with. The tactic involved creating a vanguard with the shield ships and battleships next to one another. If they got it together, they'd charge, blasting at the Emancipated fleet all while in the protection of their front line vessels.

The Emancipated fleet shared the same configuration. All their crafts came from the same blueprints. Precious little was different but the minor changes, the weapons and the way they used them, tended to set the two cultures apart. If they allowed the Founders to prep up their attack, it might turn the tide of the conflict.

"We have to stop that," Raeka said, pointing at the screen. "Get the scouts on the line and have them harass the ships who haven't formed up yet. They can't let up until we're able to make our own push or we might lose this fight. In fact, get some of the damaged ships to fall back. If we are routed, I don't want anyone left behind."

"Yes, sir." Tarkin replied, leaning to speak into his microphone.

My opponent knows if he gets in that position, we're done. He also knows I can't let him. That means he probably anticipates my attack with the scouts but I don't have a choice. It's either that or flee and we can't give up now. This might well be one of the final battles for our people. If we wipe them out here, they won't have much left to fight with.

The scouts engaged, firing wildly into the fray. It caused some chaos but battleships returned fire. Raeka's stomach sunk when he saw one of his scouts get annihilated but the others evaded and moved out of range again. The formation continued to build. Raeka gripped his hands into tight fists.

"One of the scouts has volunteered to sacrifice themselves," Gahlir, the communication's officer, announced loudly. "They are willing to initiate a self destruct sequence and fly into that formation."

Raeka struggled with the offer. Part of him agreed, it would be a sound tactic and likely throw the Founders into disarray. However, just shy of a hundred people crewed one of those vessels and at least some of them would die. If they started bailing out before picking up speed, the enemy might redirect and make the sacrifice pointless.

I'm responsible for so many deaths already...but if we don't make this sacrifice, will I be responsible for losing that many more? This is why we need peace. Decisions like these should never be made and wouldn't be necessary if the politicians spent more time analyzing the cost of their war, and less arguing over inconsequential grievances.

"I..." Raeka sighed. "Give the order. Allow them to perform the attack."

A bright light flared off to the right, cutting through the window and filling the bridge. Raeka winced and rubbed his eyes, dazzled by the suddenness of it. *Is that a new weapon? Did the Founders develop something we didn't know about? Impossible! Our spies would've caught it.*

"What was that?!" Milana, his pilot asked the question but he had no answer. He turned to Gahlir.

"What do you have on scans?"

"I...don't know what to say...it seems..."

"Well?" Raeka spoke impatiently. "Hurry, man. What do you see? What did they fire at us?"

"They didn't...it...well, it's a ship."

"What class? Is it reinforcements?"

Gahlir shook his head. "No, sir...it...just appeared. Literally, it wasn't there a moment ago and now...poof. It's there."

"Impossible." Raeka waved his hand. "You must be mistaken. They just used some sort of device to get in quietly. Now, what class?"

"Sir, I'm putting it on screen. It's vastly larger than anything the founders have to field. Believe me, I've never seen it before...nor do I understand what I'm even looking at. The design, the materials, the hull...none of it matches anything in our databases. Honestly, I'd call this an alien vessel."

"Aliens? Preposterous…" Raeka's sentence died on his lips as the scan came up on the main screen. Indeed, the massive craft looked nothing like anything he'd seen before and it proved to be absolutely *massive*. It began to drift, hovering slowly among the stars. No light emanated from it. Perhaps it was a husk, a craft from some long dead age…but he still struggled to believe it.

I feel like I must *be dreaming*. "Can you hail it?" Raeka asked. "Are you picking up any signals at all?"

"I'm scanning the surface now but the material is defying our scans…" Gahlir paused. "I'm picking up a low level energy reading but little else. Hm. Sir, there's something on the side of the ship. Some kind of sigil or marking. Perhaps it represents a designation of sorts? I'll enhance and magnify."

"Thank you." Raeka rubbed his chin. The Founders fleet fell back, disengaging from the fight and his fellow captains allowed them to. They gave up the attack formation as well. *Curiosity trumps conflict I suppose.* Little stopped a battle besides attrition and supplies. Many fights ended as a result of running low on ammunition long before both sides were decimated.

Which is why the war rages on. If one side or the other would simply take the fight to the other's world, fully commit their forces...but the risk was too great. If the gambit failed, then they'd have nothing to defend with. Raeka privately believed both sides feared destroying one another, ending their existences completely.

"On screen now, sir." The screen flickered, pulling Raeka's attention back to the present. He squinted, taking in the strange characters. B E H E M O T H. He'd never seen such a thing but perhaps they could interpret.

"Run that through the universal translator," Raeka said. "And let's get a scout over there to check it out. So far, it's not acting in an aggressive manner so let's collect as much data as we can. Everyone stay on point and get me the Founder captain. I'd like to see what their intentions are in light of this situation. I'm thinking this may call for a truce."

After Dawn knows we could use a minute to breathe.

Chapter 1

Captain Gray Atwell's ears buzzed. Confusion gripped his mind as consciousness trickled over him. Pins and needles danced through his limbs as a muffled beep mirrored the hammering of his heart. He opened his eyes, peeling the lids back from sandpaper eyes. Misery increased exponentially as he drew a deep breath and stirred.

What the hell happened? The first thought after waking up made him roll over on his back. He stared up at the ceiling of the bridge, a blurry gray mass of metal. Someone else moaned off to his side, expressing their discomfort audibly. The sound turned Gray's stomach. He'd barely acclimated to the annoying *beep*...which must've been an alarm.

Okay, so we're probably in trouble. Get up, Gray! C'mon! Get up!

"Captain?" Ensign Paul Bailey's voice helped root him in reality, bringing his senses back fully. "Captain, can you hear me?"

Gray nodded. "Yes, I can...I'm here. What's going on?"

"I'm not sure. I came to help you up." Paul gestured behind him. "I couldn't wake up Renee...he's still in the pilot's seat but unconscious. Mac's also down in Navigation."

"Christ…" Gray shoved himself up, holding onto Paul until the darkness receded from his vision. "Did our jump go bad? Are we home?"

Paul took his seat again and tapped the controls, shaking his head. "Looks like we're on auxiliary power only. All my connections to the rest of the ship, engineering, medical and even scans are offline. Nothing seems damaged but the generators are off. I can't raise anyone on the com either."

"I'm sure everyone just experienced the same fate as us." Gray sat in his own chair and checked his computer. It was working but the network was down. He wanted to get up and check on the other members of the bridge crew but his legs didn't immediately respond. Taking a moment sounded like a good idea. "What can you get done from your post?"

"I can try to establish a connection to the rest of the ship's systems, those that can operate on low power mode. The network *might* be able to come back online but I'd really rather have Olly help with it."

"I'm going to get down to medical, you hit engineering. We'll need both up and functioning if we hope to fix this." Gray rubbed his eyes. "You ready for this?"

"Yes, sir." Paul nodded.

"Link back up in fifteen minutes regardless but if they're waking up down there, see if you can help them get the generators back up."

"I'll do what I can. Good luck, sir."

Gray watched the younger man go and drew a deep breath. His limbs still felt heavy but he did his best to shake it off before heading down the hallway. The elevators were offline as well and he suddenly didn't envy poor Paul. Engineering was several decks lower than medical. They both had some exercise coming either way.

The first few rungs didn't bother him too much but after two decks, Gray started sweating. Whatever knocked him unconscious did a serious number on him. He felt like he just recovered from the flu, especially the way his stomach started flopping around. When he arrived on the deck he needed, he leaned against the wall in an attempt to recover.

Jumps are hard on the body as it is but this one…God, I hope we made it home. Maybe they'll send some help when they see us drifting out here. So much for a flawless mission.

Gray shoved away from the wall and stumbled the first few steps before steadying out. By the time he reached the sick bay, he found others sitting up and crawling to their feet, looking as disoriented as he felt upon his own awakening. Doctor Laura Brand leaned against a computer console, tapping at the panel.

"Doctor?" Gray cleared his throat.

"Captain!" Laura glanced in his direction but didn't move. "Thank God you're okay. We seem to be having a power problem. Is that something you'll be able to help with?"

"Paul's gone to Engineering and I came here. How're your people?"

"Recovering. I haven't done a full analysis yet, but it looks like whatever happened effected our equilibrium. Unless I'm mistaken, I think it'll wear off on its own but...judging by your grim expression, we don't have time for this to happen on its own, right?"

"Pretty much."

Laura nodded. "I'll work on a compound to hasten the process as soon as I determine exactly what happened. It would happen a lot quicker if I had access to the network and my computer equipment."

"Like I said, we're working on it."

"Have a seat and I can check you right now."

Gray began to protest but decided against it. He felt a need to wander the ship and check on people, Adam, Clea...the rest of his senior staff. But if he collapsed in the hallway, he wouldn't do anyone any good. He moved over and took a seat near Laura and leaned back, his body relaxing the moment he took the weight off his legs.

The doctor waved a device near his chest and checked the results, staring intently at the small screen. After a moment, she performed another pass. "The network might be down but our hand held units are designed for leaving the ship. They won't give us the same deep diagnostic I'd prefer but they'll do for now."

More crew members started pouring into the sick bay, various people rousing to seek help. Each person who entered increased Gray's relief. Hopefully, there were no fatal casualties. *I have to ask Clea how often this type of thing happens to an Alliance ship. Ours is having serious issues*.

One of the com units nearby started to chime and Laura tapped it. "Sick bay, Doctor Brand speaking."

"Hello, Ma'am," Paul's voice piped through the speaker. "I'm sorry to bother you but is Captain Atwell with you?"

"He's right here." Laura turned to Gray. "Go ahead, I'm still going over the data I collected."

"What's going on, Paul? What did you find in Engineering?"

"Controlled chaos, sir. Something happened to the pulse drive. I've managed to rouse Chief Engineer Higgins and we have a small crew up and functional. They're going to focus all their attention on restoring power."

"Good." Gray frowned. "Did you encounter anyone else on your way down there?"

"Yes, sir. Many people were moving about and heading for one of the medical bays. I considered finding Lieutenant Darnell and seeing if he can help with the tech station on the bridge."

"Good idea. Olly was off shift so I'm guessing you'll find him in his quarters. Unless he already woke up. Head over there. When I'm done here, I'll head back to the bridge. Contact me there."

"Yes, sir." Paul killed the connection.

"Why is communication working?" Laura asked. "If we're down on power?"

Auxiliary maintains absolute essentials. Life support and communications are both on that list. The latter because we need to be able to talk to one another to fix the problems." Gray stretched. "What's your prognosis?"

"You're fine," Laura replied, drawing a glare from Gray. "Oh, you wanted more?"

"After what I just went through, yeah, I expected something else."

"Your body is in the process of recovering from shock. A full shift of rest would fix the problem. However, I know you don't have that kind of time so I'm going to give you a stimulant combined with some nutrients. The combination will buy you several hours but you're going to need rest."

"When we're mostly recovered, I'll take your advice." Gray rolled up his sleeve. "Until then, let's make this happen."

Laura left him alone for a moment to prepare the shot and he stared off into space, contemplating the next several hours. Engineering already jumped on their first priority. The Behemoth at least needed backup power. That would engage several systems making it possible to fix the engines.

They also needed to figure out where they ended up. Did the ship get home? Lieutenant Timothy Collins, the navigator, should be able to go to astrogation to determine their position. They used it for star mapping, a concept Clea stated was aboard every alliance ship. Once Gray knew Tim was okay, he'd send him there right away.

Establishing long range communications also fell into the essential task bucket. He took a deep breath and closed his eyes. Sleep sounded like such a fantastic idea, especially with the queasiness still gripping his stomach. Discipline made him sit forward and fend off exhaustion then Laura pierced his skin with the shot.

"Ow…" Gray scowled. "Some warning would be nice."

"I find the surprise approach tends to work far better. Besides, you looked deep in thought. I didn't want to interrupt any plans you might have for saving us all. I've seen that expression before and it tends to mean you've got a good idea."

"Sadly, I'm just prioritizing what we need to do...no good ideas, just reactions." Gray sighed. "Thank you, Doctor. How long before this stuff kicks in?"

"A few minutes at most. Take it as easy as you can."

"I have to climb a ladder all the way back up to the bridge," Gray replied. "How easy is that?"

"Um...sounds awful." Laura frowned. "Do be careful, Gray. We can't afford to lose you. Can't you just run things from here?"

Gray shook his head. "I need the resources up there. When backup power's restored, all the computers will come back online. Coordination is easier with my terminal."

"Take a break every two decks then," Laura suggested. "Might make it easier and you won't overtax yourself."

"I probably didn't have a choice on that matter. See you soon...keep up the good work. Oh," Gray paused, "essential personnel should receive the same shot I did. We'll need to get at least one good shift out of these folks before we all collapse from exhaustion."

Laura nodded. "Yes, sir..." He knew she didn't like the idea but at least she had the sense to keep the complaint to herself. They didn't have a lot of options. This was an extreme situation and it required some sacrifices. Of course, if they happened to be drifting near Jupiter, they probably didn't have much to worry about but Gray had a bad feeling they were somewhere else.

In Alliance space? Enemy territory? Neutral? So many options...I hope we find out before it's too late.

Back on the bridge, the drugs kicked in and he felt more like himself. He tried waking the others and put a call out for a medical team to make their way to the bridge when they wouldn't rouse. While waiting, Gray busied himself by checking systems with his computer, cataloging what they needed to work on.

The bridge communicator began flashing, indicating a variety of messages in coming in from all over the ship. Gray checked the intercom and cursed when it proved to be down as well. He sent a quick blast message with what little information they had: auxiliary power only, engineering was working on it, medical bay can provide updates.

Laura won't be thanking me for that later but at least she can explain what's happened to them all better than I can.

Gray rubbed his eyes and returned to his station. He had a text message from Timothy, stating he was on his way to astrogation to determine their position. Gray sent along his approval and thanks. The young man proved to have initiative many times before. This just solidified him as one of the better officers on board.

"Captain?" Gray jumped, surprised by Clea An'Tufal's voice. She didn't look too bad considering what happened. Her purple-black hair remained perfectly in place and she didn't have the dark circles under her silver-blue eyes Gray expected. "Sorry, I didn't mean to startle you."

"You move like a damn cat," Gray grumbled. "Anyway, I trust you're feeling okay if you ventured up here."

"Yes, sir." Clea moved over to the tech officer station and began tapping at the console. "I trust Lieutenant Darnell has been contacted?"

"Paul's going to find him. Do you know everything that we're dealing with?"

Clea nodded. "Yes, sir. I got your message. Seems strange to me...a jump should not have done all this. We're dealing with a much bigger problem than an FTL disaster."

"That's our luck, huh? Are you sure this isn't just a fringe possibility? One of the risks one takes in hopping through the speed of light?"

"Not that I've ever read about," Clea replied. "And note, I've read extensively on the subject."

"I'm sure you have. Do you have anything?"

"No, there's no power to this station." Clea stepped away. "I'm heading down to engineering. I should be able to help them get the generators back online quickly. By that time, hopefully Lieutenant Darnell will be up here. He can start rebooting the various systems for us. But we'll need a pilot...is he okay?"

Gray shrugged. "I've left him there just in case but medical's on the way. As you can imagine they're a little busy."

"Of course. I'll keep you informed of our progress. See you soon."

Gray watched her go. Once again alone, he felt a tickle of dread touch the back of his neck. He didn't tend to give in to pessimism but something seemed different about this situation. If what Clea said was true and this was not a normal malfunction, then what could've happened? One answer seemed obvious: sabotage.

But why? Why on the way back to Earth and not sooner? Why allow them to finish the mission at the mining facility if they intended to cause catastrophic damage? All these questions would be answered once they found the person. There were few things Gray found more reprehensible than treason and this certainly qualified.

If they didn't die from their actions, we'll find out what they're up to.

Lieutenant Commander Stephanie Redding stepped onto the bridge followed closely by medical personnel. She stepped over to Gray as the others provided aid to the unconscious folks on the bridge. "Captain." She offered a salute. "Reporting for duty."

"Not much you can do right now, Redding but have a seat when you can. I have a bad feeling you're going to have your work cut out for you once we get power back online."

"Yes, sir." Redding waited patiently as they took the others off the bridge, using harnesses to take them down the ladders.

We have GOT to get elevators back ASAP!

Communications flowed through the ship but the central relay from the bridge wasn't available to route them when necessary. The Behemoth crew operated incredibly well when their technology functioned properly and they seemed to be doing an admirable job without it but Gray knew the inefficiencies had to be annoying.

"Captain?" Clea's voice pumped through the speakers. "Can you hear me?"

Gray tapped his com button. "I can! How'd you do that?"

"We've restored one of the primary generators and are working on the others now. Engines are in the process of rebooting. Pulse drive sustained minor damage but we're already in the process of bringing it back online. The jump module...will require more time. Full power will take a while but at least elevators, communications and computers will be back momentarily."

"Great job down there," Gray said. "Is Maury working?"

"I'm here!" Maury Higgins answered. "I just let her do the talking. I'll give you status reports as they come in. Clea's heading back to the bridge I think."

"Thank you, guys. I appreciate it." Gray patched into the crew quarters area where Oliver's room was. "Paul, if you can hear me, get to one of the wall coms and report in."

A moment later, he received a connection from the younger officer. "Hello, sir. This is Paul."

"Did you reach Olly?"

"Yes, sir. He's gone to the medical bay to receive his shot and will be on the bridge momentarily. I'm going to join the tech crew to start working on repairing the systems that overloaded during the...well...the event."

"Okay, thank you."

The event. Gray couldn't think of a better term for it, at least not yet. Whatever they experienced certainly qualified. Circuits all over the ship gave out, burned by the sudden surge in power, the same surge strong enough to take all the generators offline. Of all the scenarios he played out in his head, the ship becoming disabled outside battle only peripherally occurred to him.

Plenty of accidents might occur in space. Obstacles and strange radiation bursts were only two of the many dangers waiting out there for the unwary. Gray remembered back when they planned to leave the solar system just before the first attack. Every man and woman who were part of the mission had to meet with a therapist and watch videos about space travel.

They reminded him of old driver's education videos put on for children. They long since ceased to show those horrific segments but some still survived. Many people caught them online, uploaded and restored to the highest quality such ancient footage was still capable of. Accidents and mayhem were supposed to give students a proper respect for what could happen if they weren't responsible behind the wheel of a car.

The space versions talked more about proper airlock protocol and ensuring everything was secured in your quarters at all time. Even with artificial gravity, back then the scientists didn't fully trust their inventions. No one wanted anything to float off only to crash down and hurt someone when a key system was restored.

Gray went through those videos skeptically but sitting on the darkened bridge, waiting for the elevators to come back online, he felt his mind drift back to them. *In case of an emergency, be sure you establish communications with your direct supervisor. From there, you can begin the process of repairing your vessel and saving everyone on board. Remember, safety is your duty.*

The last line always made him groan. They used it after every module as if pounding it into their heads would elevate the importance of the whole process. Most of the crews didn't buy it. They came from military backgrounds or at least, educated enough to feel like they had common sense. Even if Gray disagreed with half of them, he had to admit, some of the videos felt condescending.

"Captain." Lieutenant Oliver Darnell, Olly, stepped on the bridge. "I'm reporting for duty."

"Have a seat, Olly and be grateful they got the elevators working before you came up here." Gray smirked. "Believe me, it was no picnic."

"Understood." Olly flopped in his chair and winced. "Sorry, sir. I guess the shot hasn't kicked in."

"Don't worry about it. I think we're all allowed a little fatigue right now. Especially those of you who were on downtime." Gray glanced at his computer. It read offline still. "Clea said what they were doing would let us have elevators, computers and proper communications. Let's get stuff rebooted so we can start tallying the damage."

"Yes, sir. I'm on it." Olly paused. "I'm getting a message from Tim. He says he's got some bad news."

"Lovely," Gray grumbled. "Let me guess, astrogation is gone?"

Olly shook his head, "no, sir...but he stated we are in uncharted space. None of our maps match up with the current star configuration but um...it gets worse."

"I can't wait to hear."

"I'm patching him through the speaker." Olly paused. "You're speaker hot, Tim."

"Thanks," Tim's voice echoed in the bridge. "I'm in astrogation now, working on relative position, sir. We're in an uncharted solar system with fourteen planets. I'm trying to find...well, anything to give me an idea where we're at."

"Do you have any tech working there?" Gray asked.

"Basic computers, sir." Tim paused. "And those are running offline. I'll need to get these systems back to perform some long range scans of surrounding star systems I think. Oh...hold on a moment."

Gray rubbed his eyes. He normally had exquisite patience but today, he struggled. Tim wasn't wasting time but his research would indicate where they were and how they might get home. But without tech, they were stuck there. Without a position, they wouldn't even know what direction to *try* to go.

"Sir," Tim spoke up. "Um...we have approaching ships."

"Excuse me?" Gray's brows shot up. "Repeat that?"

"There are four ships on approach. Not fast, but definitely steady. None of their profiles match any vessels I've seen before. I ran them through the computer. They're small...probably scouts. In other quick news, there's no debris to worry about drifting into, not for a *long* way out at least...just an asteroid nearly two-hundred thousand kilometers off."

The bridge operated on screens rather than transparent glass. They were blind up there until sensors came back online and they could transmit the camera shots. Astrogation had a massive window both on the roof and on the wall outside the ship. It was meant to provide astronomers with a real view of what they were studying.

So we're drifting, ships are approaching and we're somewhere totally new. Well...it could be worse. They could've fired on us by now.

"Olly, will you get sensors back up when you reboot the computers?"

"Maybe, sir...probably. They don't require *too* much power to operate."

"Good." Gray stood up. "Tim, can you do what you have to from the bridge? If the terminals come back online, I mean."

"Yes, sir. I'm on my way."

Gray turned to Redding. "Stephanie, you ready to right us?"

"You give me engines and I'll do a barrel roll, sir."

"Okay, we should have something shortly." Gray checked the time. They were most of the way through third shift. "Let's hope we're operational right around the start of fourth shift. Keep the reports coming, folks. I want to know the moment a key station is back up. Sounds like we've got a lot to do."

Chapter 2

Raeka knew the Founder captain well. They'd fought on many occasions but never managed to take the other down. In some ways, their rival became a dangerous game, one neither side seemed capable of winning. Draw after draw marked their record, one side losing more than the other in every engagement.

When are we going to give up this senseless fighting? Today. When an alien arrives and interrupts another attempt to kill each other.

Darm appeared on the screen, wearing a very similar uniform to the Emancipated officer. They came from the same place and didn't deviate much from aesthetic. Raeka's counterpart donned red hair similarly short but he was shorter and much broader of shoulder. He worked out in a very different way.

"Is this some sort of new Emancipated trick?" Darm instantly started in with the accusations, but Raeka couldn't blame him. He thought the same thing at first.

"We haven't the technology to field such a giant," Raeka said. "And I do not believe you do either. We have sent our scouts to check it out."

"Why didn't you contact me first? We would like to send some as well."

"By all means, feel free. But you didn't answer our hail immediately and I had to take action. This thing could be a threat to both our planets, not one or the other."

"And you hope to coax them to your side, is that it?"

Raeka sighed. "Do not be daft, Darm. This is serious. Do you honestly think I'm going to attempt to subvert...you know, I'm not even going to finish that sentence. It's absurd and I know you better than that. We are talking right now because I believe we must work together. This is far more important than you or I or even the battle."

"How so?"

"Imagine what it could mean if we have proof of intelligent life beyond our sector. This is tremendous. Bigger than space travel or colonization. It might just be something that could unify us again, put an end to the war."

"You're naivety is ridiculous," Darm waved his hand. "You think learning of neighbors would settle the disagreement between us?"

"No, but if we start talking about them we might start talking about other things too. You *must* be weary of the fighting. How long before we simply…run out of people to kill each other? How long before those people realize it might happen and stop? Wouldn't you rather be the solution to a problem than the constant reason it's perpetuated?"

"If your so called government would acknowledge our sovereignty, the fighting would end."

"Why can't *your* government partner with us? We did it once but you have to admit, the taxation and demands on our resources became unfair. You didn't care whether or not we survived, only if you got your cut. That's why we pushed so hard and that's why the fighting started. Your greed created this war."

"Enough!" Darm shook his head. "We are not going to agree here on this topic so we should simply get on with the current dilemma. This new ship."

Raeka felt his spirit sink for a moment but he nodded. "As you say. Send your scouts to join ours. Can we consider this an *official* cease fire?"

"Yes, I am transmitting my seal to you as proof. Do the same. I'll instruct my crews to work with yours. No tricks, Raeka…or this will be the last time we speak in such a civil manner."

Darm killed the connection and Raeka shook his head. "Transmit our seal," he ordered. "And let me know when we receive his. Keep in contact with our scouts. I want a report as soon as they are within range to perform a deep scan."

"Captain," Tarkin turned in his seat to address him. "Did you mean what you said about the conflict?"

"About negotiating peace?" Raeka asked. "Yes, very much so. We were meant for more than war and battle. All the disciplines which put us in space have been placed on hold, my friend. Exploration, discovery, the sciences...all are directed to weapon's development and better ways to end our former home world."

"Does this mean...you'd rather us *lose*?"

Raeka shook his head. "Of course not. Remember your philosophy. A wise leader considers all obstacles, not only the one directly before him. What created the block in the first place should be one of your primary objectives. *Peace* is the way to win this forever. Both sides will have to make concessions...but my fear is neither side will be willing."

"Don't you feel we've given enough to them?"

Raeka smiled. "Tarkin, this is an old debate typically waged between *civilians*. You and I both have seen enough as military men to know what is truly meant by concession. The one thing both sides must acknowledge is the other's right to survive. We can build an alliance from that, one which is beneficial to both sides. Now, focus on your station. We can talk more about politics later."

Providing our guest doesn't decide to destroy us all when it wakes up.

***

Clea leaned over a computer terminal, reading through diagnostic reports from the various engineers working on restoring the ship. Maury tapped her shoulder. "So, I think someone may have tampered with the jump drive. I'm getting some pretty strange readings that I've never seen before."

"Keep it offline for now," Clea said. "If something catastrophic happens to it, we'll be stuck here for a *very* long time. Even at top speed, it might take years to return to Earth space depending on where we ended up."

"Our second generator is online. Darnell's rebooted the computers and we're limping back toward minimal efficiency. Scanners should be up soon."

"I'm going to head to the bridge then," Clea replied. "Let me know if you need anything and I'll support you from there."

"Thanks, we'll keep up the good fight."

Clea rushed down the hall to the elevator and struck the number for the bridge. Leaning against the wall, she rubbed her head, fighting off the fatigue clinging to every joint and nerve ending. The shot Doctor Brand came up with wouldn't have worked on her and so the medics worked on a substitute.

She'd been fast asleep when the event happened and when she came to, she was lying on the floor. She'd taken a knock to the head and a bruise formed just above her left eye. Luckily, the throbbing subsided but unfortunately, it gave way to the full body shock everyone else seemed to be suffering through.

So much for getting back to Earth quickly.

The cargo bays were full of Ulem but at least a freighter headed back to Earth with a shipment. Any more delays in getting the Behemoth's sister ship online would not go over well with the council there. They already complained about how the alliance was treating them. Any more ammunition would simply offer more chances for damaging their relationship.

After all we've done for them too...I find it unbelievable that they would continue to think of us as anything other than benevolent.

They'd learn. When they finally engaged in galactic politics and saw the full theater of the war, they'd know why they needed to trust *someone*. Standing alone would not help anyone, indeed, it would practically be suicide. They could not mass produce ships fast enough to fend off waves of enemy attacks...nor did they have the manpower to lose full crews.

Not that the kielans necessarily could but they'd colonized dozens of worlds. Their numbers were nearly twenty times that of the human populations. They had resources to wage a massive campaign, especially with their other allies all over the galaxy. The enemy itself didn't seem to have anyone, not even unwilling participants.

Their zeal and hatred overpowered their need for additional people.

The elevator opened and she entered the bridge, taking her seat and tapping into her computer. Gray tapped her arm in way of greeting. She nodded her acknowledgement but didn't look up. Her focus could not be distracted at the moment, not if she hoped to fight through misery *and* continue to do her job.

"Clea?" Olly said. "I've got the sensors back online and I'm about to turn on the monitors. Can you check my work from there? I don't want to short anything out if I got something wrong."

"Of course." Clea checked his figures, running them through an analyzer. They came back green. "You're good, Lieutenant. Go ahead and bring them back online."

The screens flickered to life and Gray stood, squinting at the displays. Clea noted a massive fleet some distance off with four vessels close by and another three on an approach vector. They didn't seem to be aggressive, not yet but sensor sweeps would tell one way or another. She assumed Olly was already on it.

Tim showed up and took his post, his fingers flying over the console. Like the others, he didn't have much to say. Even with the shots, the humans were still not entirely themselves. Hopefully, as they worked their physical ailments would subside. Clea certainly needed time to do some healing.

"I need some sensor time," Tim said. "Can you spare a couple, Olly?"

"In a second," Olly replied. "I'm getting a full read out of those ships approaching. Do we have shields yet?"

"Environmental only," Clea said. "Weapons and defenses are offline until we get at least one more generator back up. Right now, we can't even launch fighters. The hangar bay door controls were burnt. Technicians are currently replacing the damaged circuitry."

"So you're telling me we're basically defenseless right now," Gray said. "At least we have armor."

"These ships have the equivalent of conventional weapons," Olly said. "These seven could lay into us for a couple hours without causing any real damage."

"Probably not true of their entire fleet," Redding added. "Sir, I don't have engines yet."

"The engines are almost up," Clea said. "But I advise patience."

"Oh?" Gray asked. "Why?"

"Because at the moment, we're not a threat to these people. To them, we're a derelict alien vessel drifting through their space. If we suddenly turn on our engines and move, they may decide they should attack us rather than try any diplomacy. Besides, we are quite a ways from any planet or moon. We're not drifting into danger."

"Good point." Gray nodded. "Olly, do you think they know you scanned them?"

"That depends on how sophisticated their own equipment is. Pre alliance tech on Earth would've told us and they seem a *little* more advanced than we were then."

"Fair enough. Where's Agatha?"

"Probably in sick bay," Tim said. "There was a massive line, sir."

"Clea, take communications for now." Gray returned to his seat and got on the intercom. "Commander Everly, please contact the bridge immediately."

Adam Everly, the ship's first officer, would've normally been the first person to take the bridge under any other emergency. Clea knew the captain must be worried about him, probably wondering if he'd been hurt. Depending on what state people were in during the event, anything from a fall to being hit by falling cargo was possible.

Clea wondered if they lost any crew to the jump disaster. The possibility was certainly there and as she took control of the communication station, she saw dozens of concerned messages dancing across her console. People asking after friends and coworkers, wondering who made it to sick bay and who was still unaccounted for.

We'll know soon enough but a roll call is not at all a bad idea. She initiated a quick ping to all personnel, asking them to check in with their supervisors. Of those, she asked to give a missing person's report to her station where she'd tally the results and relate them to the captain. Eventually they needed to sweep the ship and find anyone missing, the injured and sadly, the possibly dead.

"Clea, do you have coms up and running?" Gray asked.

"Aye, sir. The generators have allowed for short wave coms and most minor systems."

Gray nodded. "Hail those ships. Let's get to talking."

"Defenses are online," Olly announced. "I can raise shields whenever we need to."

"Good." Gray turned to Clea. "Let me know what you get on there."

"Working on it...they may operate on a frequency or technology we do not understand. This may take a moment. I'll keep you informed."

The elevator opened and Commander Everly stepped in, using the wall for support. Gray met him half way and shook his hand, expressing his relief to see him. Clea needed to brief them both on what she heard from the engineer but it would have to wait. Talking to the foreign vessels took priority.

"What's going on?" Adam took his seat next to Gray. "Have you figured anything out?"

"Just that it involved the jump drive. Let's get Maury on the line and see what he can tell us."

That's not going to go over very well, Clea thought. *I should've told him about the potential tampering right away but it didn't exactly seem pertinent given what we were going through.*

"Maury, it's Gray. I'm with Adam on the bridge. Do you guys have any idea what happened to the jump module?"

"It's screwed up big time, sir," Maury replied. "Someone must've tampered with it. I'm still investigating but Clea asked us to keep it offline til we figured it out."

"Good call." Clea felt Gray's eyes on her. "What do you think it's going to take to repair it?"

"Not entirely sure yet...we have to open it up but right now, we're still busy trying to get regular systems online. Once we're back to standard operating health, we can focus on the jump module."

"Sounds good," Gray said. "Let us know if you need anything."

"Alright, thank you, sir."

Gray turned to Adam. "So there you have it. Tampered. A saboteur. I'd worried about that but had a hard time believing it. Now, it seems we have some evidence."

Adam agreed. "What's worse is if we don't find out who did it, they can just cause more trouble somewhere else on the ship. Maybe next time, they'll be more successful...if blowing up the ship is their plan. They clearly don't have any sort of self preservation either. What they did...Christ, it could've killed us all."

"Exactly." Gray hummed. "I've got the bridge, Adam. I want you to start an investigation. Figure out who did this and get them locked up. We can't afford another disaster, not when we've got so much going on right now."

"Aye, sir. I'm on it."

"Keep in touch with me through our *private* coms. Our traitor might be monitoring public conversations."

"Okay, I'll let you know if and when I find anything out."

Adam left the bridge just as Tim spoke up. "I think I might've pinpointed where we're at. "When I do, I'll plot a jump course home…for whenever we get the module back up. There are at least two inhabited planets in this system as well…one a little harsher than the other but definitely capable of sustaining life."

"Must be where our visitors are from." Gray hummed. "What else do you have, Tim?"

"I don't know. The fifth planet's giving me some strange readings…maybe it was subject to some kind of environmentally devastating attack. Some parts are completely uninhabitable but others read exactly the same as the fourth planet. That shows a considerable amount of industrialization."

"They may have terraformed it," Olly suggested. "And aren't done yet."

"That's possible too. Still, both of them have a lot of people. Can't get much more without moving in closer."

"Interesting," Gray said. He joined Clea at the com terminal. He lowered his voice to barely above a whisper. "Do you have anything yet?"

"No, sir. I'm broadcasting on all frequencies. We'll see if that works."

"You knew about the tampering."

"Only just. We were a little busy and it didn't seem pertinent to the situation." Clea looked up at him. "I am sorry. I would've told you when we weren't moving at full speed."

Gray nodded. "As far as priority reports go, sabotage should be considered top of the list. Going forward, if you hear evidence of that again, definitely tell me right away, are we clear?"

"Yes, sir. Perfectly."

Gray patted her shoulder. "Thanks."

Clea let out a breath as he walked away, kicking herself mentally for not informing him sooner. She felt like a right ass for being quiet but it really didn't seem as important as getting things online. Then again, a passing comment would've sufficed. She shook off the self chastisement and went back to her job.

***

Raeka stared at the screen so intently his eyes burned. The waiting grated on his patience, especially considering the severity of the situation. Part of him felt as if they needed to go weapons hot and challenge the vessel. He already received reports they would not respond to their requests for communication.

Is this a derelict? A dead ship drifting through space? If so, how did it appear out of nowhere? No, some technology is at work here but what? And is it safe for us.

"Sir," Gahlir broke his concentration, "I've received some readings back from the scouts. It's quite possible that the visitor received some catastrophic damage from their arrival here. However, we *have* discovered additional power sources on board."

"So they're recovering…" Raeka rubbed his chin. "Why wouldn't they respond to us though?"

"Perhaps their communications are not online as of yet," Tarkin offered. "If they suffered enough damage to lose propulsion, then subsystem issues would not be unheard of."

"If they power up and see our scouts," Milana offered, "then they may not be particularly happy. Without a conversation, these beings may take our approach as hostile."

Raeka considered the pilot's thought and hummed. It was possible but surely they wouldn't think such a thing with the mainstay of the fleet remaining behind. Still, considering the sheer size of the ship and what it represented, perhaps an aggressive approach made more sense. He knew his Founder counterpart believed it.

Perhaps they could disable the vessel rather than destroy it. Taking out their engines, which seemed to be situated in the aft, made sense. Then, they'd not have to worry about an attack. Communication would be on *their* terms and any negotiations from a position of power would come out better.

If we can damage them. The hull already is proving to be of material we've never seen. And what of their power sources? If they return to full functionality before *we take out their maneuvering capabilities, then there's a fair chance they'll wipe us all out.*

"Sir, the Founder fleet is moving," Gahlir said. "They seem to be heading for the alien vessel!"

"Get Darm back on the line," Raeka barked. "Now!"

Darm's face appeared a moment later. "What is it?"

"What is it?" Raeka shook his head. "What are *you* doing?"

"We are approaching the alien vessel," Darm replied. "Our scouts indicate that it is massing power and we need to be in position if we are going to offer up any sort of meaningful resistance."

"You realize we have not even *spoken* to them yet, right? This act of conflict may not even be necessary."

"Would you rather be in a position to destroy them should the need arise or sitting back here, well away from any sort of action?"

Raeka couldn't argue with his logic but he still felt they would get into trouble closing in on the ship. He rubbed his eyes, thinking through a variety of scenarios, trying to decide how best to approach the Founder captain. Would he even be willing to listen to reason? Was there a point to pushing? Or should he just go along with the plan and move in with his own ships?

I could push that we remain in reserve…but he won't go for it, will he? He'll think we might stab him in the back. The fact he started moving was meant to force my hand. I have few options that don't involve abandoning the field and in this circumstance, I cannot afford to do so. Command would have a fit.

"Very well," Raeka said. "We'll proceed with you and find a firing solution. You take the other side and we should be in a good position to hold our visitors if they decide to become hostile."

"Do not make a mistake," Darm said. "This could well end us both if you do."

The Founder ship cut the communication before Raeka could reply and he fumed over the last words. *As if I would be the one to make a mistake. That arrogant ass is going to get us all killed. We must remain vigilant and cautious through this exchange. Perhaps we can make first contact and establish relations.*

If they did so, maybe the visitor would join their cause, help establish peace. Already, the Founders and Emancipated worked together to investigate the ship. The arrival alone did what years of hope and conflict could not. Now, if they proved to be a benevolent race without designs on conquering the system, things would work out nicely.

"Give the order for the fleet to move," Raeka announced. "Parallel the Founders and give us a firing solution on the invader. Tell our scouts to fall back and rendezvous as soon as possible. Let's not leave this to our enemies to resolve. I fear they will not represent cooler heads in a volatile situation."

***

Gray continued reading through the tallied damage of the ship and very nearly cursed aloud. Whatever happened caused pure havoc through the systems, leaving the ship in a nearly worse state than the first time they tangled with the enemy, prior to pulse technology. It wasn't any one big thing either, but a whole string of small issues building up to become a disaster.

"Captain," Clea grabbed his attention. "I initiated a request for roll call from the ship. So far, we have twenty people unaccounted for. Pilots have volunteered to help locate people and are on the task now. They'll return them to sick bay as they discover them."

"Thank you," Gray replied. "Any response from those ships?"

"No, sir."

Olly spoke up, "they're falling back." He paused. "Sir, their fleet is moving closer."

"That's a lot of ships..." Gray rubbed his chin. "What are their intentions?"

"I've had the chance to scan the area," Olly said. "I've picked up some debris and energy signatures consistent with combat...I think these ships were engaged in a fight before we arrived."

"Really..." Gray scowled at the screen. "And now they're approaching us."

"If they were fighting," Redding said, "then we may have become a force to unify against."

"Shields are ready," Olly said. "I can get them up right away."

"If they start to get aggressive, we'll raise defenses," Gray replied. "For now, we *must* get through to these people. Clea, what's the hold up?"

"I've checked for interference and I haven't found any. I think we might just be operating on a very different type of technology for whatever they use to talk to one another. Lieutenant Darnell, can you scan them for communication equipment? Maybe you can tap into it or at least show me how to connect with them."

"I'm on it." Olly went to work and sighed. "Sir, I think they might be posturing now...I'm seeing some energy build ups from the larger ships."

"Are they even within range?"

"Not effective...unless they figure we can't move anyway so might as well throw some ordinance our way." Olly shrugged. "If we couldn't defend ourselves..."

"I get it," Gray interrupted. "Raise our shields. Are the engines online? Weapons?"

"Engines, barely," Clea said. "We could probably maintain position but fancy maneuvering is out. Weapons are *not* online. I'll up their priority."

"This thing isn't about fancy maneuvers," Redding replied. "But I get you. Once we've got power, I think we can outrun those guys if we have to. And I can at least nudge us to avoid the majority of their attacks. I'll monitor progress on the weapons."

"Okay, do it." Gray turned to Clea. "Keep up the work with Olly. If we get attacked, I'd like to at least know why. Looks like we might be in the midst of an intergalactic incident with a new culture. Not exactly the first contact I hoped to be but maybe we can pull ourselves out of this yet. If only we can talk to them."

Chapter 3

"Captain!" Ghalir shouted. "The invader seems to have come alive! They have raised a shield, much like ours but...but vastly more powerful. Their engines are also up and they are no longer drifting."

Raeka glared at the screen and sighed. This would give Darm all the ammunition he needed to start a fight. The invader now represented a clear threat to the sector, one neither side could technically afford. If this joint ventured guaranteed a chance at a peace table, Raeka would've already opened fire but he knew it wouldn't.

When they finished with the invader, chances were good they'd turn right back on each other.

He looked over Ghalir's readings and confirmed them. The man was right and worse, they proved to be technical giants comparatively. Wherever they came from, they brought *vastly* more advanced equipment. Further observation was required, but Raeka's fear was they may have the power to take out *both* fleets.

"Continue your scans and get me Darm on the line. This changes a few things."

Moments later, the Founder captain appeared on the screen. "I see you've also picked up the power surge," Darm said. "Either they are about to flee or attack. I am preparing to give the order to open fire."

"Do you have any idea what our weapons will do against their shield?" Raeka asked.

"We'll find out."

"The hard way," Raeka finished the sentence. "What if they react in a strange way? We have no way of understanding this alien without *investigation*. Hostile action could well end any chance of communication."

"We'd waste time talking if they are here for a hostile reason, Raeka. You should know this just as well as me. We are working in tandem and I expect you to back us up. We will send word when we're prepared to attack. Darm out."

Raeka cursed and slapped the arm of his chair. *That fool will get us all killed!* He sighed. Part of him knew the man was right. Waiting might prove suicidal. They needed to prepare for the attack but to do so, his people had to coordinate with the Founders. That would be interesting. Many of them hadn't spoken in a long while.

Maybe through a little cooperation we'll see a change. One can hope.

***

Clea received Olly's scan data of the incoming vessels and sifted through it quickly. Most of the information he procured was consistent with her understanding of space faring vehicles. The emissions from their engines and the environmental shields matched up with different designs used throughout the alliance.

The one part that didn't match was an anomalous reading that appeared more like standard radiation but nothing on their ships should've produced such a small amount. As she analyzed it, she found a pattern and from there, she discovered they disguised their com traffic, essentially encoding it to look like ship emissions.

Once she knew what she was looking at, Clea broke it down quickly and used the universal code as a translator. It had served the alliance several times during first contact missions and it worked here as well. Their words came through, crews coordinating with one another. She came in at the middle of their conversation.

"Fire team six, do you have a good lock?"

"That's a negative, control. We're having a hard time."

"How? The thing's huge! You could eye ball an attack from this distance. Other fire teams, report."

Clea turned in her seat, raising her voice as she spoke, "captain, they are preparing to engage us. I've got their coms."

"Lock on to that large ship on the starboard," Gray said, pointing at the screen. "Broadcast to the whole thing if we have to. Tell them we're here in peace."

Clea locked on to the vessel and sent a broad communication, using their same technique. It probably caused tremendous feedback through their speakers for the first few moments before leveling off. She spoke into her microphone, calmly and in a professional tone of voice.

"Incoming vessel, this is the Behemoth. We represent no threat. I repeat, we come in peace. Please do not fire or engage. We have no cause for conflict."

She held her breath in anticipation of a response but when none came immediately, she repeated her message, this time more firmly. This time, she received a message back immediately and the com translated for her in real time.

"Behemoth, this is the Emancipated Flagship Endiras. I'm putting you through to my captain, Raeka Anvinari. Please hold."

Clea rolled her eyes. "They've put me on hold, sir."

"You have to be kidding." Gray came to her console, clenching his fist. "Why?"

"They're patching me through to their captain."

"Put it on screen. I'll talk to this guy."

"Yes, sir."

A moment later, a man appeared on the screen with short, dark hair and nearly black eyes. His pale skin stood as a sharp contrast to his darker features and he looked almost sinister. A scowl crinkled his brow and he tilted his head, as if examining the people he saw on the screen.

For all intents and purposes, they looked somewhat similar. Humanoid, like the kielans. Clea watched Gray to see his response but he maintained a neutral expression.

"Hello," Gray began. "My name is Gray Atwell, the captain of this ship and we'd really like to avoid any aggression. We didn't mean to trespass. We had a malfunction and it led us here. If we can't treat peacefully, give us some time and we'll happily leave your space and never return."

"I am Raeka Anvinari, captain of the Emancipated fleet. You represent a common threat at the moment, one two sides of a conflict can rally together against. Tell me more about this malfunction and how you came to be here in the first place. Our sensors stated you simply appeared out of nowhere. Explain."

"We have faster than light technology," Gray said, "which allows us to cover great distances almost instantaneously. In this case, something happened to it and we're temporarily without the ability. I assure you, we mean no harm to either of your fleets so you don't have to rally against us. We'd be happy to talk if you choose to be amiable to conversation."

"You picked the correct vessel to speak to," Raeka replied. "My counterpart would not have answered you. He believes in taking no chances, no risks. Our culture has been at war for quite some time, you see. Any peculiarity may be seen as an attempt by our enemies to subvert and destroy us."

"Understood but surely you both know we're not on either side. The fact we don't speak the same language, our tech is different…you've scanned us, I'm sure. You know we have advanced defenses and weaponry by now. Even our engines are more potent. I don't want to get into a fight we can avoid."

"I get the sense you're not saying this because you're afraid." Raeka smirked. "I appreciate you have not overtly threatened us but we do recognize your technology. Do you think you can take on both fleets?"

Gray smiled back. "Let's not find out."

"I should tell you, when we separated from our home world after they unfairly began to exploit us, we vowed we would never be taken in by words again. Somehow, we've become the more reasonable of our two factions. Though we originated from the same place, a schism formed. One of entitlement versus a desire for freedom."

"We have a similar story from our past," Gray said. "Eventually, the two became allies and worked together."

"A hope I've fostered for some time," Raeka sighed. "You seem to not be a threat but...it will not be an easy sell to Darm."

"Let's get on it then," Gray said. "Conflict is not in either of our interests."

"I will get him on the line," Raeka replied. "And contact you back."

Clea cleared her throat. "They have cut the connection, sir."

Gray nodded. "Let's keep scans and shields up, Olly. Let me know if you detect any energy build up. I want to know before they try to lay into us."

"Yes, sir..." Olly glanced over his shoulder. "I haven't figured them out yet but I'm probing their computer systems. It may be possible to hack them and take control. Their security protocols are somewhat primitive."

"A good option," Clea said. "Be careful with the Universal Code, however. If even a fraction of it ends up left behind, they can adapt it."

"Don't worry, I know how to get in and out of places I'm not allowed..." Olly sighed. "That came out wrong."

"Just focus on the task at hand, Lieutenant." Gray shook his head. "Now, let's hope Adam's having some luck with his investigation."

***

Adam left the bridge and headed straight for the engineering deck. People raced around him, filling some of the corridors to the point he needed to take detours to get to his destination. The controlled chaos aboard the ship annoyed him. Whoever proved responsible for the sabotage would definitely feel the full weight of his ire.

He checked his computer as he walked, noting the injury list. Five people were found dead already and two more weren't expected to survive their injuries. Not only did the tampering cause the ship to arrive at the wrong destination but it destroyed several lives. No one had time to worry about it at the moment but when things slowed down, it would definitely affect morale.

A thought occurred to Adam as he walked. The jump module acted up when they performed microjumps. There was a possibility, however slight, that this was an accident and *not* the cause of a saboteur. He didn't want to believe it, not with how angry he felt but he couldn't rule it out completely.

A witch hunt when technology was to blame didn't make much sense.

As he arrived, he stepped into a room full of tension but relatively quiet. The men spoke firmly to one another but no one yelled. All the stress came from their postures and the severe expressions they wore. Each man and woman focused on their tasks, dedicated to restoring the ship as quickly as possible.

Maury approached him. "Commander, I didn't expect to see you down here."

"I'm here on the captain's orders," Adam replied. "Can we talk privately for a moment?"

"Absolutely, we can use my office." Maury led him across the engine room to a small attached room with a sliding metal door. Inside, a meticulously clean desk was bolted to the floor. Shelves were covered with metal slats to keep books and other trinkets from falling and a few pictures hung here and there, depicting Maury's family. "What can I do for you?"

"Tell me about the jump module," Adam said. "Have you been able to perform a diagnostic?"

"Only cursory," Maury replied. "We can definitely repair it but it'll take some time."

"How much?"

"I'm guessing six to ten hours just to be safe. Mistakes could mean leaving it in an irreparable state."

Adam nodded. "What did the cursory diagnostic tell you is the problem?"

"The jump module taps into the crystal powering the drive," Maury explained. "There are essentially tuners inside that are perfectly aligned to channel the vibrations required to make a jump. Honestly, to get any more detailed about that part, you'd need to have Miss An'Tufal explain but ultimately, those tuners are out of alignment and the power junction box was shorted out."

"How could that happen?"

"A serious jarring," Maury offered. "It's not common wear and tear. Those tuners are tough in one regard but not hard to manipulate. I expect you're investigating my concerns of tampering. It's more than possible. Someone with a strong arm and a pair of pliers could screw up the tuners. The power relay wouldn't be hard either—a quick jolt at the right voltage would do it."

"Who all has access to the engine room?"

"My entire roster of engineers, of course," Maury replied. "The captain, you, Miss An'Tufal and the highest ranking security personnel."

"And how hard would it be to get any of this done under the noses of your staff?"

"We staff heavier during second and third shift. Forth is the lightest unless we're in the midst of an operation. During that time, it would be far more possible for someone to do something unnoticed. However, we have sensors for that sort of thing, measures to catch people in the act of performing unscheduled maintenance."

"How's it work?"

"Let's say a tech finds a problem with the engine stabilizers. He can't just grab a wrench and go to town on it. He has to log his findings and schedule his work. Then one of the supervisors approves it and he gets it done."

"And in the case of an emergency?"

Maury nodded, "I thought you might ask. We still have to log it which is just as easy as using your communicator to record your findings. However, even in an emergency there are some systems which are only available for higher ranking personnel to get into. A junior tech would not have access to the jump module."

"What if I tried to just bust it open and go to town?"

"It would cause an alarm to go off through this entire deck as well as in the quarters of all senior staff. We would receive com messages as well."

"I see. Can you send me the one offs you're talking about from security? I have the rest."

"Right away." Maury tapped into his computer and sent the information over. "There you go. Why do you think someone would do this?"

"I don't know. It was suicidal either way. If it worked the way I expect they wanted it to, we should all be dead."

"What's your next move?"

Adam smirked. "Best if you don't know. I'm going to take a look at the jump module then run some scenarios. Mind if I use your office for a bit?"

"Not at all." Maury gestured. "I'm getting back to the pulse drive. We're doing some testing to ensure we're ready to move without blowing up."

"Good idea. Double check any critical systems for tampering as well. There's a chance this wasn't the only trouble they tried to cause."

"Yes, sir. I'm on it."

Adam went to the jump module and ran a scan on it. The most recent access came from one of the senior technicians who ran a diagnostic on the system. Before him, Clea looked at it and before that, Maury did a check during the action around the mining station. No one logged a maintenance request in the last twenty-four hours.

He went to Maury's office and shut the door, checking the security footage of the area throughout the shifts leading up to their jump. Many people went in and out but the computer identified them as people who belonged. The next set of footage made him frown. The area around the jump module was also under observation however, a large chunk of footage was missing.

He found that three hours before the jump until just after were simply gone. Someone had deleted them from the system, essentially protecting themselves from getting caught performing the sabotage. Whether they did it alone or had an accomplice, Adam didn't know but they had to be good with the computers.

An edit to security footage would've triggered an alert to the tech officers and security as well. Adam checked the log and neither department received a message about this anomaly. The error catalogue also didn't indicate anything out of the ordinary. It was as if the system believed everything was fine, despite the missing segment.

He looked up the security personnel who had access to the engineering room and looked through each record. Nothing jumped out as suspicious to him but he'd have to talk to them all to be sure. His mind started formulating a theory though, one which pointed directly at Clea An'Tufal.

After all, her sister turned traitor, why not her? And the captain liberally allowed her access to her sibling during their trip back. Adam wondered how often they spoke after the woman was put in the brig but when he checked, he found Clea never visited the security area during that trip.

If she's to blame, it must've happened before. Or perhaps after.

The why didn't make sense. Clea didn't seem easily swayed by rhetoric and her discipline was too great to assume she'd just *decide* to become chaotic. Besides, she also seemed to enjoy living. Suicide through jump drive malfunction sounded ridiculous. He rubbed his eyes and considered the evidence again.

Clea looked like a great option because the evidence specifically pointed at someone with her expertise. What he needed to do was find another person with similar skills, a person who might well be able to pull of the same types of technical marvels and get away with it. There were a few key points to consider.

One, the person who performed this sabotage assumed it would not destroy the ship. Otherwise, they wouldn't have covered up their crimes. They'd be dead. Two, whoever pulled the crime knew the protocols of the ship intimately enough to be thorough and save themselves getting caught before the event took place.

However, Adam refuted the first of his two points because they might not have wanted the alliance to catch on who pulled the act of terrorism. After all, there could be a mastermind behind the attack and whoever did it could eventually be caught. That would take a high level of paranoia and confidence in where they'd appear though so he deemed it unlikely.

And two remained strong. The person definitely knew their protocols well. That made security personnel sound likely but would they even know how to open the jump module? He didn't see how they would or why. Unless someone was cross trained. Everyone on board the Behemoth was required to pick a station to cross train.

Adam went through the security personnel again and found a young man who had done just that. He graduated infantry but his secondary job involved repairs. He even helped out during the engagement near the research facility. This guy had the ability and skill to pull of the repair part but hacking the computers, he didn't seem to have that background.

Still, Adam knew he had to interview him and the others as well. He needed to pick up the pace so he could find out what happened in time to stop any other problems they might be facing soon. This meant getting back to his own office and scheduling some meetings. He contacted security and got two soldiers to meet him there.

He'd need some help securing folks during their talks. If he found the perpetrated, he wanted to have him put into custody immediately. There was no time to lose.

***

Raeka paced as he waited for Darm to appear on the screen. The visitors seemed entirely too reasonable to start a fight with them and their technology may well be more than enough to destroy both fleets single handedly. Whatever happened in the next twenty minutes could spell doom for both sides.

When Dark finally appeared, he wore an expression indicating severe displeasure at being interrupted. He crossed his arms over his chest and scowled, his jaw tight.

"What exactly do you need, Raeka? I'm busy preparing to launch an all scale attack on that ship."

"I've been in contact with the visitors and they have made it quite clear they are not here for violence," Raeka explained. "They have offered to share their culture with us or, if we would rather not, they will also leave peacefully. I believe we should allow them to depart without hindrance."

"Are you insane? They are playing you, man!" Darm shook his head. "I thought more of you as an opponent but you are truly naive. If we do not strike while we have the upper hand, they will surely destroy us! Don't you see that?"

"I think if we force their hand, they will defend themselves. We'll be guaranteeing losses instead of chancing their deception. Besides, if they could kill us and were willing to do so, why wait to play us? What benefit is there?"

"Do you not have xenology classes on your world? The home world offers such education and the universal truth is simple: you cannot trust the mind of an alien. They do not think like us and they cannot. They come from not only a different culture and world but environment with its own unique impacts on their systems and brains.

"No, we cannot chance this, Raeka and we need your help if we plan to take them out. Believe me, this is the only way to ensure the survival of our species."

Raeka considered what Darm said for a long moment. Some of it rang true, even though it defied his instincts. Captain Atwell seemed like an honorable man, willing to work with them. Rational even. But if they were thinking strangely, if for some reason they took a perverse glee in building a rapport before attacking, then Darm was right: they should strike immediately.

He considered his men on the bridge for a moment, wondering if he might be doing a disservice to their families by not removing this threat. Sometimes, he found himself a bit liberal about the intentions of others. He considered all beings relatively good until they proved otherwise but maybe this time, that was a bad idea.

He sighed and nodded his head, coming to a conclusion. Darm was right. The better choice was to not be sorry. He needed to get his men and women home safely. Leaving their lives to the chance that the visitor was good didn't make sense. He wanted to believe them but the warning could not be ignored.

Advanced as they were, as dangerous as they appeared, Raeka realized destroying the Behemoth might well be their only chance to survive. He sat in his chair and leaned back, feeling his stomach perform flips at what he was about to do. He turned his attention back to Darm and nodded again.

"Alright, Darm. I agree with you." Raeka turned to Tarkin. "Weapons, come online. Finish preparations and wait for our mark to fire. After Dawn help us…this could very well get messy."

Chapter 4

Olly continued rebooting minor systems throughout the ship, letting the maintenance happen on his left screen while keeping the scans up on the middle one. Much of the stress lifted from him after the conversation with the alien fleet. He figured if they kept their word and talked the others down, the Behemoth could get underway back home soon.

The fact the two fleets planned on attacking them disturbed Olly. How could they come to such a conclusion? To destroy a vessel without even trying to talk to them seemed psychotic. What if they were simply disabled? They could've needed help but instead of rescue, they would've been hammered by a barrage of ordinance.

Oh well, they didn't do it so we're all good. Even if they decide to attack us now, it won't work out for them very well. Our shields are online. If only weapons were up, we'd be golden.

Olly shifted his attention to the generators and checked the progress. Everything was nearly back, the guys downstairs really worked their butts off. He checked to see if they had enough to get the cannons up but the computer calculated they needed at least ten minutes before they'd be operational again.

He ran a scan over the other ships in the area to see how long their shields could fend off an assault from them. The results made him tilt his head. They seemed to be surging, as if they were powering up to be used. *This doesn't make any sense...I mean, they said they were going to stand down. Or at least, they planned to talk to each other.*

But the readings were unmistakable: they were about to be attacked.

"Captain!" Olly spoke far louder than he meant to but he didn't feel bad about it. "They're going weapons hot, sir! They're about to attack!"

Gray stood up behind him. "What? Did you just say..."

"Yes, sir! They're powering up right now!"

"Shields?" Gray asked.

"They're up and have full power..." Olly paused. "Or close enough to it. Ninety-eight percent."

"Clea, get that guy back on the com."

"Sorry, sir." Clea sighed. "They're not acknowledging our hails."

Gray joined Olly at his station. "Where're we at with weapons?"

"They're not ready yet...Computer showed roughly eight minutes."

"Can we handle them hitting us for that long?"

"I was just about to evaluate them when I caught what they were doing," Olly replied. He tapped over the keys for a moment and nodded emphatically. "We *should* be fine. They're conventional weapons. Our shields will pretty much ignore them but...a seriously prolonged bombardment won't do us any favors."

Gray turned to Redding. "How's the helm? Can you maneuver?"

"Yes, sir. We have some movement."

"Okay, if they start shooting, let's keep moving to give them different sections of the shield. They'll probably try to surround us. Start falling back. We might be able to outrun them."

Clea spoke up, "if we go full throttle, we can ram them all and take minimal, if any damage. However, most of them would not survive. This will buy us plenty of time for repairs and departure."

Gray turned to her. "I'm surprised to hear you say that. It's a pretty harsh tactic."

Clea shrugged. "We have limited options and they've proven to lack reason. After a conversation, they've decided to not stand down. While our weapons are nonfunctional, ramming is a valid tactic. If you recall, our enemy uses it to great effect."

"Yes, but they don't care if their ships explode." Gray shook his head. "No, we're not doing that...but we'll hold them off until a better option presents itself."

"Diplomacy sure isn't working," Redding muttered. "I hope they listen when we have guns again."

"Works if we show them off," Olly replied. "And I'm trying to route more power to get them up. Engineering complained but I let them know what's going on. They calmed down quick."

"I bet." Gray sat back down and rubbed his eyes. "Let me know right before they're about to fire...we'll address the ship and let them know. I can't believe this situation went south so fast. Maybe Raeka couldn't convince the other commander...either way, I hope we're able to. If we have to destroy all these ships, we won't exactly be making a good first impression."

***

Adam received the message about the imminent attack after he returned to his own office. He'd just started to follow a new trail, trying to determine who on his suspect list may have been in the engine room around the time of the sabotage. Unfortunately, none of them checked in if they did show up. He'd have to ask the techs on duty to see if they remembered any unexpected visitors.

When the alarm sounded, his first instinct was to rush to the bridge to help. Unfortunately, they were hip deep in extenuating circumstances so he second guessed and sent a quick message to Gray asking if he wanted him to drop the investigation temporarily. The captain replied quickly with *no, keep looking. We need to find the traitor as quickly as possible.*

Luckily, the security personnel would not be busy with battle stations, not as much anyway. When he brought them in, they might be particularly stressed because of the fight going on but they wouldn't be key to any sort of operation aboard the ship. He dialed up the best suspect, the young man with the tech skill and security authorization to do the deed.

Lieutenant Joseph Keller joined the crew with countless others. He had an above average rating on all of his fitness exams and performed his duties more than adequately. Every CO he served under praised his critical thinking and wit. By all marks, a fine officer probably up for promotion in a few years time.

Adam didn't know the man personally but he'd seen him around. Captain Whitney Garrison was his current direct CO so Adam contacted him for a quick chat. This man might be busy with something to do with the action about to take place so the conversation would need to be quick.

"Captain Garrison here," the crisp greeting spoke of years of service and saying that exact line a million times. "What can I do for you, Commander?"

"Hi Whitney." Unlike Joseph Keller, Adam knew the Captain well. He'd worked on several projects for the executive staff and always came through when it came to ensuring security details were handled professionally and properly. Most of Adam's interaction with him came from before the Behemoth. They'd served together for a while. "Are you in the middle of anything pressing? I don't want to keep you."

"I'm just getting the security crews ready to keep an eye on key locations around the ship," Whitney replied. "I've got a quick moment."

"What can you tell me about Joseph Keller?"

"Keller?" Whitney sounded surprised. "Um...he's a good kid. Works hard. He's studying to become an engineer. Really wants to fix the pulse drives and stuff. Joined the infantry as a way to get his foot in the door and have his school paid for."

Adam hummed. "Nothing out of the ordinary with him? No strange complaints or issues with the military? Or even the alliance?"

"No..." Whitney paused. "What's this about, Adam?"

"The event," Adam replied. "I'm investigating the possible and probable sabotage of the jump module."

"Oh wow...I doubt it was Keller."

"Why? Do you know if he has an alibi?"

"I don't but I mean, I can't see him doing it. He's pretty apple pie patriotic, you know?"

"Yeah, I get it." Adam thought for a moment. "Whoever did this either had help or knew how to hack the security console to erase a chunk of time from the camera. Can you guys investigate that? See if there's any log of someone getting in there?"

"Sure, how serious is this?"

"We're afraid whoever caused this trouble might've done something else. As we find ourselves turning back on systems, we might well cause more damage because of tampering. I need to get to the bottom of it, even with this impending attack."

"I understand," Whitney said. "I'll get on this personally and contact you back as soon as I've had a chance to deep dive."

"Thanks," Adam replied. "Talk to you soon."

Adam turned back to Keller's file and read through his personal information. He was born in Florida and grew up less than five miles from headquarters. His father worked for the military as a liaison with contractors building various parts for space craft. His mother stayed at home.

He scored well in high school and even better at the academy. When he graduated, he could've gone into many different tracts but *picked* infantry. It wasn't necessary and that made Adam scratch his head. A smart guy like Keller could've gone into engineering early on. Why change paths now?

Adam sent a request for Keller to come to his quarters and let the two security guards outside know he was on his way.

The explanation in the file stated he wanted more challenging work. No doubt true all things considered but it should've happened earlier. How far back could this conspiracy stretch? Adam didn't think it could possibly have started before they launched the ship. Whoever did this work was given the order sometime between departing to liberate the mining station and just before the jump catastrophe.

Maybe a transmission was received, something encoded. Adam brought up the communication logs and had the computer search for any messages to Keller. It found a missing time block of an hour just after they arrived near the mining facility. *A whole hour? That's a lot of data! How did no one catch this?*

He explored that problem and discovered why. A cursory look at the logs showed steady communications but getting specific made it point out blank entries. There were actions, but they zeroed out—a point which required scrutiny to catch. It would've been caught in a scheduled audit but by then, the ship would've been destroyed.

But again, if the person was trying to blow us up, would they have cared about that? Or did they really think someone would find us and perform some forensics to discover this stuff?

Adam knew he was looking for a computer expert, someone who knew their procedures just as well as the technical specs of their systems. Maybe Darnell could help…if he wasn't involved. Adam checked the young man's alibi and he was dead asleep during the deletion of the coms. The computer confirmed his location and state.

What about Clea?

A knock at his door distracted him.

"Sir?" One of the guards peeked in. "Lieutenant Keller is here."

"Thanks, send him in." Adam observed the young man as he entered. The lieutenant sported a short hair cut, making him nearly bald but for the sprinkle of brown decorating the crown of his head. He had a wide jaw and blue eyes, almost a poster perfect infantryman. As he stepped closer, he snapped to attention and offered a crisp salute.

"Lieutenant Joseph Keller reporting as ordered, sir!"

"At ease," Adam said. The man settled into a more comfortable stance. "I'd like to talk to you about some recent activity down in engineering. Someone tampered with the jump module and erased the camera footage of the area. What do you know about it?"

Joseph's military discipline gave way to surprise. "Sir?"

"Do you need me to repeat the question."

"No, sir...but...I don't know anything about it."

Adam checked the computer for Keller's whereabouts during the time period. He was *not* in his room but it didn't say where he was. "Can you tell me what you were doing at the end of second shift and the start of the third?"

"I was on duty on second," Keller replied. "And went to the rec room after things settled down and we were jumping home."

"What did you do?"

"Watched a holovid with Corporal Vandon."

"Which one?"

"*Late Moon*, sir." Keller blushed. "It's a horror movie, sir."

Adam checked the computer to see what played during the time he mentioned and it came back true. Corporal Vandon was also not in his room during that period. The rec room itself showed multiple people but they didn't check into the area and didn't need to use their IDs to open the door. Vandon would have to corroborate his story.

"What did you do afterward?"

"We chatted for a while about the vid...we thought it was stupid. We talked about going to the mess hall for chow when the jump happened and I woke up on the floor. I took Vandon to sick bay."

Adam checked with medical admittance and had to give them credit. Even during a catastrophe, they maintained strict discipline with their procedures. Vandon and Keller checked in at the same time. Vandon was treated for a minor head wound. Keller received the shot and got cleared for duty.

I think this kid must be innocent.

"I need you to submit your com device for inspection." Adam held out his hand. "Now."

"Yes, sir." Keller pulled it off his belt and handed it over. Adam downloaded his contacts and every message he sent and received for the past three days. He handed it back.

"Thank you for your cooperation, Lieutenant. You may return to duty."

"Sir, permission to speak freely."

Adam considered the request for a moment before nodding. "Granted."

"Do you feel that I'm responsible for this?"

"You fit the perfect profile, Lieutenant. I had to be thorough with my investigation. At this point, I'll be reporting to the captain that I don't believe you had anything to do with this."

"Will any of this go against my permanent record?"

Adam lifted a brow. "No, this won't be on your record at all. We need to find whoever did this, Lieutenant. They may have done more and we can't afford that now. Any moment, a fleet of low tech ships is going to begin bombarding the Behemoth. While we can take it, the problem comes when we try to do anything about it."

"What do you mean, sir?"

"Just this: what if they tampered with the weapons? Or the shields? Whoever messed with the jump module might've been subtle with other systems. And they had an accomplice. There's no way they could erase the footage, turn off the alarms *and* perform the sabotage. We might have a whole group."

"Or one person with a firm understanding of automation."

Adam frowned. "Explain."

"If they planned well in advance, they may have written a program to initiate these various tasks when they needed them. They'd be bound pretty specifically to a time frame but anyone able to do what we're talking about would know the schedules of all the people in Engineering. One highly skilled person could definitely pull this off, sir."

Fantastic, Adam thought. *I'd figured Olly or Clea or a group. This kid picked apart the potential plan. Who? The roster doesn't show anyone with the potential who wasn't accounted for. It couldn't have been a senior staff member. I just don't believe it.*

But why not? The idea, reprehensible as it may've been, seemed perfectly possible and logical. Maury definitely could pull it off if he had to. But wait...couldn't someone else have forged the computer to say they were in their room? Olly probably could. He looked up at Keller. "You're dismissed, Lieutenant. Thank you for your cooperation."

"Yes, sir." Keller saluted again and left the room.

Adam patched into Paul's com unit. "Ensign Baily, do you read?"

"Loud and clear, sir," Paul replied. "What can I do for you?"

"I need to know something. Where did you find Lieutenant Darnell when you went to help him out?"

"He was in his room, sir."

"In bed?"

"Well, on the floor technically."

"How was he dressed?"

"For rest period," Paul replied.

"State of the bed?"

"The blankets were on the floor…" Paul started to sound worried, suspicious even but he didn't ask.

"Thank you, Paul. You can get back to your duties."

"Yes, sir…"

Adam killed the connection and rubbed his eyes. He hated having to distrust their own people, to wonder who he could trust and who might be a traitor. They'd been through a lot together, these men and women, and to think any of them would betray the trust of the entire crew felt unthinkable.

I can't wait to ask this criminal why.

He knew no answer would suffice. There were no good reasons to risk lives. Terrorism, perhaps, but even that just explained a motive. No, someone was behind this and he felt like it might be the alliance. Maybe he needed to go further back in his research to when the prisoners were aboard…

But their cells *never* opened for the duration of the trip from the research facility back to Earth. He double checked the logs and did a quick deep dive to prove out no more tampering and it came back clean. *What about during the prisoner exchange?*

He watched the video of them marching Clea's sister off the ship and she never left the custody of the guards. It couldn't have been her. Besides, someone had to *physically* tamper with the jump module and considering how they did it, it wouldn't have worked to get them to the mining facility.

So Adam found himself back to square one, thinking about what might've happened in the last twenty-four hours.

The ship shook. Those idiots outside finally attacked. *I hope these fools realize quickly they can't take us. This is going to be a dark day if we have to destroy a fleet on our first contact* and *arrest one of our own. Can't wait to hear what the council will have to say about all of this. Those prigs will probably...*

Adam sat up straight as a thought occurred to him. The Council. Some of them were downright ornery about the alliance. A few of them flat out hated the tentative relationship developing between humans and kielans. Could one of them have something to do with this? *Talk about paranoia...but it's another lead. One I need to follow. I need to check on Clea's location too. Got distracted by Keller.*

Adam brought up the security footage of her floor just before the jump and for the hour prior. The logs had been deleted and the security footage was offline. *That's a little suspicious but she's a great scapegoat if the people trying to do this want to raise suspicion about the alliance. And if you can delete one set of security logs, you can delete them all.*

He brought up personnel files and began sifting through. Someone must have a connection to the council. Someone with the talent and skill to commit treason. He just had to find out who...why could come later when they ensured no other damage had been done. Then, if he proved to be right, they could deal with the real threat after returning home.

***

The attack began suddenly, a barrage from every ship almost perfectly in sync. Gray had to admit the idea was sound. Hitting the shields at precise locations should've made a difference. Weaken one point and punch through, tear through the hull and find sensitive systems to destroy.

Fortunately for the Behemoth, their shields were far too powerful. That didn't stop his heart from racing when the first blasts struck them. Despite *knowing* the outcome, his heart didn't necessarily believe his logic. He checked the readings and found the shields to be operating within perfectly acceptable limits.

We're fine for now.

"Olly, weapons?"

"They're getting closer, sir." Olly sounded just as frustrated as Gray felt. "I'm still trying to get into their computers but they're so low tech, it's harder than it should be."

"Permission to withdraw," Redding said.

"Denied," Gray replied. "Running now will waste power and frankly, I believe we can win these people over."

"The weapons may not be the best way to make friends," Clea said. "Speaking from a strictly diplomatic point of view."

Gray shook his head. "Sometimes you don't have to shoot someone to prove you're scary. Olly and Tim, find me a space body, something big."

"Like…a planet?" Olly asked. "A moon?"

"Not *that* big." Gray peered at the screen. "An asteroid…something like that."

"Okay." Olly performed the scan and turned in his seat. "We've got one nearly sixty thousand kilometers away."

"It seems to be a stationary body," Tim added. "Something that's probably been in slow orbit for a *long* time."

"Redding, can you hit it from here?"

"Not easily, sir...I'd like to get a *little* closer at least."

"Move us out then and get us within range. When we've got weapons, we'll give them a little demonstration." Gray stood up and looked over Olly's shoulder. "If that doesn't get their attention and give us a bargaining chip, then I guess we'll have to make it more extreme. I want a count down for weapons, Olly. Put it up on the screen to the left."

"Yes, sir. Three minutes to minimum power, five to optimal."

"Sounds good." Gray returned to his seat and took a deep breath. The ship began to rumble as the pulse drives propelled them on, moving starboard to avoid running into any of the attacking ships. Contact with a single one would obliterate the vessel and probably kill anyone on board. They didn't have the structural integrity to handle a collision course.

Clea was right that such a tactic would've ended the fight immediately but Gray couldn't bring himself to do it, not yet. These people deserved one last chance to come around and be civil. If they chose not to, that would be their business. Earth history was already littered with situations where people were terrible to one another upon their first meeting.

Gray hoped that space travel might change that. Just once, he'd like an exploration mission to end with positive results. If he had anything to do with it, they would not become murderers, even in self defense. As the invaders, they needed to continue to show good intentions and by not attacking, they'd definitely grant this new culture some perspective.

I just hope it makes sense to them and they back down. They seem like quite the proud race of warriors. God knows how most of them like to finish a fight. Providing they don't take the Spartan ideal of death is glory, we should have a good chance to come out of this as friends. Come on, Raeka. Read the intentions of my next move properly. I don't want to be the instrument of your death.

Chapter 5

The two fleets could not maintain a constant state of fire, not all at once. Their first attack was everything at once, an attempt to overwhelm the defenses immediately. When that didn't work, they took turns so the shields constantly took *some* damage. Gray admired the theory. If they didn't let up, if they could keep it up, they *might* come out ahead.

Redding moved them into position for their little demonstration. The motion put the attackers on alert and they started to scatter. Perhaps they feared the tactic Clea suggested. Surely their scientists figured out just how bad it would be if the Behemoth chose to ram them. Perhaps if this new culture put together that the Behemoth neither opened fire nor chose to crush them, they might become amiable to peace.

"We're in position now," Redding announced. "I've targeted the asteroid and am waiting for full power to the weapons. It's a big one, sir. I'm of the impression it might be better to cut it in half rather than obliterate it. The debris might cause some serious problems in the system...depending on how they defend their outposts, of course."

"Good idea," Gray said. "Split the main body then one of the halves. That should be a sufficient show of strength."

Redding turned to look at him over her shoulder. "Sir, if that does not work, shall I input their ships into targeting? A few of the smaller ones."

"Only when the time comes," Gray said. "If you do that and they detect the lock, it might undo the whole point of our demonstration."

"Yes, sir."

Gray looked at Adam's report flashing on his screen. He wanted to see what his first officer had come up with so far but he needed to remain focused. The attackers might not be able to hurt them per se but anything could happen. They might even turn to extreme tactics like the enemy, ramming *them* with a few vessels.

Even atomic cores could do serious damage. That might be the only way their fleets could cause real damage to the Behemoth. Maybe if they had every ship their planets ever built, they would likely be able to to take them down. But out here, in the middle of a battle where they probably already lost a few ships, Gray felt mostly secure in this conflict.

"Weapons are up!" Olly shouted. "Engineering is ninety-seven percent online!"

Gray turned to Redding. "You heard the man. Open fire."

"Firing now, sir."

Olly put the asteroid up on the screen. Their pulse cannons fired, precise shots at key locations indicated by the computer. In an instant, the rock began to splinter then drift into two halves. Redding tapped her console and fired again, this time cutting a second piece into a large chunk. Only minor debris went flying off in various directions, nothing nearly as bad as if they had obliterated the asteroid completely.

The display was nothing short of extraordinary. Though not nearly so large as a capital ship, the rock definitely had some density to it. Even a cursory scan would prove that out. Most importantly, it *looked* dramatic. As it separated, seeming in slow motion, Gray felt the immensity of the action, the sheer magnitude of it all.

Now, they needed patience. The attackers would need a few moments to realize what they just witnessed and to fully embrace what it meant to them. If they didn't respect the Behemoth's restraint, then they really were lost. Gray needed to make a choice at that point: take them all out or flee.

"They aren't slowing down," Olly said.

Gray hummed. "I noticed. What the hell..." He turned to Clea. "Broadcast a message to them. Tell them that was just a demonstration of what we can do. Let them know the asteroid *could* have been one of their ships. Remind them of our *peaceful* intentions."

"On it, sir." Clea returned to the com station and spoke quietly while Gray considered the situation further.

These cultures must've come from a dark place to be so determined to destroy them. Their level of distrust and paranoia put them on par with the enemy, or so he believed. Not since some of the more zealous warrior races of human history had a group been so determined to waste their lives in a pointless display of courage and foolhardiness.

Gray connected his com. "Engineering, update on the jump module. How're we doing with repairs? We could *really* use a rapid extrication right now."

"Sir, this is Maury. We've established that there's nothing preventing us from opening the device and fixing it now. We're working on it now but it'll take at least a few minutes. Getting those tuners aligned properly is the difference between getting home and being lost in space...again."

"Okay, give me frequent updates. I want to the minute status." Gray turned to the others. "Jumping might be an option soon. Tim, do you have coordinates yet?"

"Yes, sir. Sorry, it's on your computer since we've been so busy with other things."

"No problem." Gray leaned forward in his seat. Fatigue gnawed at the back of his neck. The shot must've been wearing off but he didn't have time for it. Forcing back the feeling of discomfort, he remained focused on the task at hand. Whatever came in the next several minutes might make the difference between being friends or enemies.

"Maybe that asteroid was sacred," Redding offered. "We might've just blown up their version of the Egyptian pyramids."

"Not helpful, Lieutenant Commander," Gray muttered. Privately, he knew she was right. If the asteroid had been there for a long time, and these people were particularly superstitious, they very easily could've annihilated something they held dear. He knew other cultural faux pas from Earth's history that resulted in violent misunderstandings.

Maury's latest update stated they were almost done getting the tuners aligned but would need to run a couple diagnostic tests in order to ensure they were prepared properly. He estimated another ten to fifteen minutes of frantic work before they could leave. Gray nearly cursed aloud. They didn't have that much time before these people got even more desperate.

"Redding, get us turned around and start falling out," Gray said. "Let's put some distance between us and them until Maury gets the shields back up."

"Sir, we could still unleash fighters," Clea announced. "They might be able to disable their ships without too much damage."

"No engagement," Gray replied. "Let's just get out of here."

***

Raeka hated what they were doing. Watching the constant barrage of their weapons hammer the visiting ship, he felt like they were little more than children swatting at a giant. He wished Darm would've listened to reason but that fool would fight to the bitter end. When the Behemoth unleashed their own weapons and destroyed the asteroid, he felt sure Darm would pause.

Instead, he upped the urgency and hit them harder.

The only man who tries harder after having his nose flattened into his skull.

As the Behemoth powered up and began to turn, Raeka knew they were planning to flee the area. They would depart and avoid further conflict, once again proving their words of peace. How could Darm think they *still* wanted trouble? He couldn't help himself and decided to raise the man on the com again to work it out.

"Darm, you're being a fool," Raeka called out. "They are *retreating*! They do not want to hurt anyone. Can you just stop being pig headed for a moment to realize that?"

"Perhaps we have them on the run…"

"You are a blind idiot!" Raeka brought his fist down hard on the arm of his chair. "Do not mistake their departure for our success! They are leaving to spare us! Now back down! Cease fire before it's too late and we miss the opportunity of a lifetime! This culture can share so much with us, we are throwing it away!"

"We can learn a great deal from their debris. Do *not* stop your attack, Raeka or we'll turn on you immediately."

Raeka stared at the screen, unable to speak for a moment. "You truly are mad."

"Determined," Darm corrected. "And committed to safe guarding our people…even yours in this case. Don't stop. We'll have this wrapped up soon. You'll see."

The communication dropped and Tarkin turned to him. "Do you want us to stop firing, sir?"

Raeka knew Tarkin agreed with him. They'd both seen enough violence in their days to know when they couldn't win a fight. Their ranks and positions proved as much. This situation they both knew would result in a loss before it even began. They should never have opened fire in the first place but now that they had, it would be difficult to sell the visitors any sort of trust.

"Not yet," Raeka replied. The comment made him sigh. "Let's see what these visitors do for another few moments...Hopefully, Darm will realize he's making a mistake."

"You realize he may turn on us the moment the visitor's ship escapes," Tarkin said.

Raeka nodded. "Yes, he's predictable in that way. When one enemy's gone, the other takes its place. I don't know how he'll acclimate to civilian life, if he ever makes it back. War is in his blood. Let's hope we don't have to spill it to get him to simmer down. Remain on target. I'm sure we'll be stopping soon enough."

***

Adam read up on Keller's admission to the academy but found his parents helped him and no one else. He had no such activity with any politically powerful individuals. Just a friendly instructor who mentored him through the last year. Otherwise, he came back clean. Though he fit part of the bill, he didn't seem to be the saboteur.

As he continued through to find others who had anything to do with politics or the alliance, he found some connections. Some of the officers who achieved higher ranks quicker had been associated with military council members but one in particular shocked him. Lieutenant Junior Grade Tim Collins worked as Admiral Torian Jameson's personal aide for over two years.

Interesting.

Jameson always proved to be an outspoken opponent to any sort of collusion with the alliance. He harbored an obvious and outward prejudice of the kielans and never trusted them, regardless of what they offered and had done. Adam heard plenty of stories from Gray about the man. The Admiral seemed to hope for failure to prove his points.

Could he have influenced Tim? But that young man always seems so level headed. I can't imagine he would've gone for something so...crazy as to sabotage the ship. If nothing else, I've always felt like he has too much self preservation to do such a thing.

Even if he did influence the navigator, the young man didn't seem capable of all the things he'd have to be able to do in order to pull off the tampering. He needed computer access, engineering access *and* he had to be able to automate things to be able to get rid of the evidence. Adam never thought of him as *that* technologically proficient. He was an astronomer first and foremost.

I'd better dive into his education though. I could be very wrong about my impression...however, there's something else to consider. If Jameson really did put an agent on the ship, he may well have had the man or woman trained off the grid and off their record. An intelligence agent pull off their duty completely under our noses.

If Keller had been acting alone, Adam would've believed the man couldn't have hidden his skill set but with the help of an admiral...the sky was the limit.

Adam performed a cursory search for anyone with a top secret clearance, something above even his or the captain's. As he expected, nothing came back but it would be too simple if it had. Tim's file showed the exact type of education Adam expected to find. He didn't touch on engineering nor did he study advanced computer techniques.

Who else got a sponsorship from Jameson?

Most officers who served aboard the Behemoth received some type endorsement. Some came from politicians, others high ranking military officers and some from highly respected civilian authorities. These were recorded in each officer's file along with the letter written on their behalf. Tim's was fairly direct.

Cadet Timothy Collins has submitted his request for a commission. Please accept my endorsement for his advancement into the junior officer's corp. As an intern with my office, he performed with discipline and efficiency. I have personally worked with him on many occasions and have total faith in his abilities.

Few men take such pride and exhibit such passion in regards to astrogation and astronomy. He can speak of the stars for hours and consistently proves he has taken his education to heart. Any ship or research facility will be lucky to take him on and shall be all the more successful as a result.

My own staff could use a junior intern of such skill and when this request is granted, I shall extend him an offer. Do please reach out with any additional questions and I will gladly answer them. Thank you for your kind attention in this matter and I look forward to seeing this young man's future blossom.

Yours, Admiral Jameson.

Many endorsement letters tended to be much longer. Adam's took up three pages but then his came from a congressman. Perhaps high military command afforded an admiral's word more stock. He probably didn't have to write a great deal because if he said the cadet deserved a commission, the board simply granted it.

I need to talk to Collins but he's on the bridge and probably busy as hell. But if he's my guy, or has anything to do with it, then he's in the perfect place to cause trouble. Adam engaged a security program to monitor Tim's console, ensuring that every keystroke and activity was recorded.

He also locked that station down so access to engineering was restricted. This left Tim the ability to do scans and lock in navigational courses...which he'd just done not long before. Adam's eyes narrowed, taking a look at the coordinates. He wasn't sophisticated enough to fully understand them, not when the origin point was somewhere entirely unknown but he did recognize the star map.

It showed Sol rather prominently and around it, the star systems charted by the alliance.

Okay, so he's at least taking us home. If he's involved, he changes his mind.

"I sincerely doubt he's got anything to do with this." Adam rubbed his eyes. "This suspicion is seriously getting out of hand."

He wrote a brief message to the captain concerning Tim. *Can he be spared for a conversation?*

A reply came back right away. *I'd be hard pressed to let him go right now all things considered. What's up?*

He may have something to do with this but I need to hear what he has to say.

Gray's reply took a few moments. *What evidence is leading you there?*

A connection to Admiral Jameson. I'm trying to target people who might have reason to put doubt in our technology or our relationship with the alliance. Not returning from that mining run might look like we were set up.

Understood, Gray replied. *I'll send him to your quarters shortly. Gray out.*

Adam leaned back and prepared for a far less comfortable interview, one which might reveal a traitor in the inner circle of the bridge staff. The thought made his stomach sink but if this was the man, then he'd be able to keep the traitor from performing any further harm. Much as he hoped it wasn't Tim, part of him wanted to be done with it.

The sooner we find him the better…even if it is painful.

***

Redding got them turned around and buried the throttle. The ship rumbled for a moment as the engines fully engaged, propelling them forward. She watched their speed carefully, worrying about the damage they'd suffered from the bad jump. The pulse drive warmed up sufficiently but she still didn't entirely trust it.

Chief Higgins insisted the only problem revolved around the jump module. Redding's stomach still felt tight as the speed increased. If something happened, if they lost acceleration, they'd have to fight. She noted the attacking fleet gave chase, trying to keep up as they departed. It didn't make sense.

What's with these guys? Are they seriously this bent out of shape that we showed up? Have they never made a mistake before?

The Behemoth could easily take them all. A quick simulation suggested it would take only a few batteries to disable them or even destroy them all. Maybe they deserved to meet their match and get taken down a notch. It might help the next poor bastards who happened upon this miserable sector.

Of course, the reality with warlike cultures was they rarely learned a lesson which changed their perspective. They merely became more convinced of their need to fight. The real enemy, the one who invaded Earth space only a few years ago, held much in common with these folks.

If the two ever met, they'd certainly have quite the exchange. Neither side would back down, nor would they accept surrender. This culture would be utterly destroyed, their resources taken and their memories wiped out. All because they didn't want to play nice when *benevolent* people showed up who could help them.

Figures that our first contact would be with total jerks.

"Captain," Olly's voice interrupted her thoughts. "We are putting some distance between us and the larger ships but the smaller ones are keeping decent pace. Of course, they are the ones capable of the least amount of damage as well."

"Throttle seems sluggish," Gray said. "Is that your impression as well, Redding?"

"Yes, sir," Redding replied. "Though I didn't bury the needle immediately either. As we reached certain speeds, I increased throttle. This gave the engines a chance to go from cold to hot without the stress of a sudden change."

"How're things holding up, Olly?"

"Internal sensors show nominal," Olly replied. "Seems all systems are back."

"Good." Gray paused. "Lieutenant Collins, please report to Commander Everly's office immediately."

Tim turned in his seat. "Sir?"

"Do you need me to repeat the order?"

"No, sir. I'm...I'm on my way."

Redding frowned, watching the navigator leave. When he boarded the elevator and was gone, she cleared her throat. Part of her said to keep her mouth shut, that it wasn't any of her business. But they were in the midst of a crisis and they might need Tim to plot a new course when the jump drive returned.

Olly took over the navigator's duties without being asked but he wasn't an astrogator. He could fake it, yes and so could Redding if it came down to it, but ultimately, they shouldn't have had to. She glanced over her shoulder to get a look at the captain, to determine whether or not he was in the mood for a question.

He wore a neutral expression.

Oh well, here goes.

"Captain, permission to speak freely?"

"Denied," Gray said.

There went that ask.

"Permission to have our backup navigator report to the bridge."

"I've already sent him a message, thank you, Lieutenant Commander."

"Yes, sir."

Why would Tim be taken off the bridge at a moment like this? What's going on?

Asking the questions internally didn't help as much as acting Gray would've but at least she gave them words in her mind. Maybe later he'd explain. She understood him keeping them in the dark for the moment. If they decided to take down the other fleet, they'd be a little too busy for a random explanation concerning a shipmate.

"Captain," Olly said, heaving a sigh. "I have some good news and bad news, sir."

"A little of the former sounds nice. Let's go with that first."

"The jump drive is operational again. Mock tests prove out we can get out of here."

"That's great news." Gray joined the young man at his station. "What's the bad news?"

"I just picked something up on long range scan. Someone jumped in hot and is moving in our direction fast."

Redding's blood ran cold. "The enemy? Here?" She shook her head. "They can't have been hunting for us. There's just no way."

"They're here for this culture," Gray said. "To do to them what they tried to do to us."

"If you're right about that," Redding said, "then they'll tear through these people. None of their ships stand a chance against two of their warships."

"I know." Gray stood, crossing his arms over his chest. "They're going to wipe out their planets, destroy these fleets and then do God knows what. Strip mine their planets? Who knows. Whatever the case, I don't think we can stand by and let it happen. Not while we're in system and combat effective."

"What do you propose?" Redding asked. "These people don't want our help. They haven't even stopped attacking us yet and there're new players on the board."

"They probably don't know about the attack yet," Olly said. "Their equipment isn't remotely as good as ours. I'm sure we're the early warning detection here."

"I say we try to talk to them one more time," Gray said. "If they won't take us up on the offer, then we have to do something. Innocent people, civilians on their planets shouldn't suffer even if their military is causing the problem. Clea, open a channel to this Raeka character. We'll make him listen and if not...well, we'll head out there and take them on ourselves."

Chapter 6

"Captain," Gahlir spoke up. "The visitor is attempting to communicate again, this time they are stating it is absolutely urgent. The lives of our civilians are stake they say and if we do not want to see our homes devastated, they say you should speak to them right away. They are…somewhat insistent."

Some nerve! Raeka raged internally. *Perhaps I was wrong about you people after all! Threatening our homes? What kind of warriors are you!*

He wanted to tell them this directly. "Patch them through. I'll speak to them right now."

"Yes, sir."

"Alright, Captain Atwell, you have my attention though I'm not sure you wanted to do so in such a negative way. Do you think this will halt our attack? Threatening our homes?"

"First off, stow that nonsense. I'm getting a little tired of your stubbornness." Captain Atwell's voice carried the same frustration Raeka felt. "Second, we're not threatening anyone. You can already tell your attacks on us are ineffective. We have no reason to cause trouble. In fact, we were about to leave your system when we picked something up on long range scans."

"Explain."

"We and our allies are at war with a culture that seems hellbent on destroying everyone they encounter. When they entered our space years ago, they destroyed an outpost then laid into our fleet. We lost all but one ship, the one I'm standing on now. If it wasn't for the timely intervention of the kielan people, our world would be dead right now."

"And you believe you've picked up these...fiends...on scans?"

"We know we have and they've already destroyed something," Atwell replied. "Do you have any way to connect with your outposts in this system?"

"Not easily, no. If they're too distant, we must travel closer."

"We can feed you the data and the historical records of our first encounter with this threat. I recommend you save your ordinance for them because they'll be here soon. You don't have long to decide whether you want to trust us or not but I tell you this: we're going to face them down either way. I won't let your civilians die, even if you're all too pigheaded to help us."

Raeka considered his words for a long moment. They proved themselves to him already but he really wished he could check on their claim of the attack on his own. Still, their historical data may be interesting, if it wasn't fabricated. He didn't believe they should be attacked in the first place. Now, he had to back down to check their story.

"Order the fleet to stand down," Raeka said. "Cease fire."

"Yes, sir." Tarkin smiled when he said it then turned to the task of issuing the order.

"I must get off the line now, Captain," Raeka said. "I need to explain to Darm why we're backing down from the assault. I don't know if he'll listen but I'll try again. Send the historical data as soon as possible. It may help our decision one way or another."

"Thank you, Raeka. I appreciate it." Atwell signed off the line. The Founder fleet continued their bombardment but, as expected, Darm reached out to them the moment their ships stopped firing. He didn't waste a moment but Raeka allowed him to wait, letting him sweat for the time being.

It would be so easy right now to convince the Behemoth to help us take down the Founders then face the enemy without them. With the power they command, they could turn the tide of this conflict, put one or the other of our sides in charge. I don't even know why I'm resisting that tactic...but I can't do it. Not if what Atwell says is true.

Raeka connected to the Founders. "What do you want, Darm?"

"I see Emancipated treachery still runs deep."

"Because we stopped wasting our power on attacking a target we cannot destroy? Wake up. There's more going on here than a visitor coming into our space. Now we have others, racing toward us and they've already destroyed one of our outposts."

"Outlandish lies," Darm barked. "I suppose you heard this from the target. Did you stop to think they could be lying? Or even worse, that they have reinforcements on the way?"

"Do you think they need them?" Raeka asked. "They could very easily wipe out both our fleets right now. You saw what they did to the asteroid. They're sending us historical data which I'll share with you but know this, one way or another, they're going to face an enemy on our behalf. The least we could do is provide them some backup."

"You're a fool, Raeka."

"No, because I see the truth before me, Darm. And you're ignoring it. Technical giants like these people do not need help to kill us and they wouldn't toy either. I've spoken to them and found they are much like us in many ways. They operate on *reason*…which perhaps does differentiate them from you."

"Your slander isn't helping win me over."

"I'm rapidly reaching the point of not caring about your opinion," Raeka said. "Now, your choices are simple: cease fire and hear them out or continue firing and risk obliteration. I've got to analyze this data now so do make your decision quickly. Raeka out."

The com line went dead and he turned his attention to the computer. Somehow, the Behemoth was able to translate the information into a format they could consume, converting it appropriately. *More wonders they could offer us but we're playing the blind man to opportunity*. He wondered how many other cultures they met who treated them with reverence instead of fear.

Raeka thought about aliens many times as a child. He remembered stargazing, wondering if anyone else might be out there, looking up at a different formation of stellar bodies. His parents never understood his fascination, often chastising him to focus on his studies and to stop day dreaming.

Years later, after joining the military and taking to the stars, he finally had the opportunity to visit the vastness of space. But instead of exploring the cosmos, he applied his creativity and wit to violence. Countless soldiers lost their lives when they went up against him and as he advanced through the ranks, it felt more and more like he would never see another solar system.

One day, my luck will run out. I'll be dead or worse...forced into retirement. What a sad end to a child's dream.

Information appeared on his screen from the Behemoth, detailing their encounter with the enemy and showing just how dangerous they truly were. As he began to take it in, he felt alarm building in his gut. The horror this enemy represented felt far worse than anything his people had ever done to each other...which was saying a lot considering how long the war raged.

Darm will have to listen to this and if he won't, we'll have to leave him behind. This could be the end of all if we're not quick to respond.

***

Adam stood up when the guards announced Timothy Collins's arrival. He intended to see how guilty the young man appeared by putting it to him pretty hard. This meant he needed to steady himself, preparing for a hard approach to someone he worked with every day. He lost the element of surprise by summoning him during combat but he felt he might be able to knock him off balance, trick him into revealing *something*.

Tim stepped inside and snapped to attention, offering a crisp salute. "Lieutenant JG Timothy Collins reporting as ordered, sir!"

"I need to know your whereabouts prior to the jump," Adam said. "What were you doing after the mining operation wrapped up?"

"Senior bridge staff had been relieved for the next shift," Tim replied. "I went to the mess hall for dinner then returned to my quarters to get some rest, sir."

"What did you have for your meal?"

"Er...a ham sandwich, sir."

"To drink?"

"Water, sir."

Adam scowled. "What did you do when you returned to your quarters?"

"Showered then watched a vid before going to sleep."

Adam checked the computer to corroborate his story. He did check into the mess hall but his quarters did *not* log his entry until *after* the event. "Would you like to explain why you just lied to me?"

"Excuse me, sir?"

"You were not in your room." Adam gestured to his computer. "You didn't check in there until after the event so explain. Why would you lie? I'm about to have you arrested for treason, insubordination and conduct unbecoming an officer."

"I..." Tim's cheeks reddened. "Sir, I..."

"Out with it, Lieutenant!"

"It's just...I didn't stay alone." Tim cleared his throat. "I was in Lieutenant Conway's room...sir."

Adam knew Theresa Conway. She worked in security. He checked her file and found she kept under the radar, mostly performing administrative duties. Her technical expertise fell in computers and surveillance. She and Tim *might* have pulled the job off together but he didn't see how she connected to it all. What motivation would she have for helping?

"How long have you been seeing one another?"

"Three weeks, sir."

"I see. And you were there all night?"

"You can check her room, sir. We both logged our entry just after the mess hall."

Adam looked and the logs did indeed show their arrival. What it didn't have was when they left. More importantly, the logs seemed to stop an hour before the event and didn't ever pick back up. Some computer glitch prevented it from storing activity. Someone may have tampered with it but Adam would need a better technician to confirm.

"Why do you think the computer stopped logging activity for that room after the event?"

"Perhaps it was a short, sir," Tim offered. "Many systems suffered similar problems all over the ship."

Adam nodded. "What's your opinion of the alliance?"

"They're...fine, sir. They saved us, didn't they?"

"Not exactly an answer...certainly a non-committal one. Do you hate them?"

"No, sir." Tim's expression altered, turning cold. It was as if he turned off all emotion.

Is he hiding something or is he just uncomfortable that I'm pushing? Time to press harder I guess.

"So you don't agree with the perspective of Admiral Jameson?" Adam asked.

"Sir?"

"I know you got your endorsement letter from him and you acted as an aide for a while. Are you trying to tell me none of his rhetoric wore off on you? You didn't find him the least bit compelling?"

"I'm not sure what rhetoric you're referring to, sir."

Adam slapped his desk. "Cut the shit, Lieutenant! This is serious and you're playing games. We both know that Admiral Jameson is a strong opponent to any sort of collaboration with the alliance. He doesn't trust them, doesn't like what they've done for us and will tell anyone who will listen how we should back out of any arrangement with them. Do you deny that?"

"No, sir. The admiral can be heavy handed from time to time."

"So what do you have to do with this sabotage?"

"Nothing, sir." Tim stiffened his back.

"What does Conway have to do with this sabotage?"

"You would have to ask Lieutenant Conway, sir. I cannot put words in her mouth."

"I don't believe you."

"I'm telling the truth, sir."

Adam stood up and paced behind the young man, giving him a moment to think about the situation. The situation became far too fishy, too full of coincidence to be let go easily. He wanted to bring the man down to interrogation and hook him up to a lie detector test but it was pretty obvious he wasn't telling the truth.

Whether he sabotaged the jump module or not didn't change the fact he was hiding something. Why bother at this point? He could save himself by speaking up. If he didn't commit a crime, keeping quiet just incriminated him. Was he protecting someone? Surely, he knew it wouldn't work out.

"Did you hack into the computer to erase video footage of the engine room?"

"No, sir."

"Did you have anything to do with altering security data to ensure someone would not be caught tampering with the jump module?"

"No, sir."

"Let me be more specific. Did you coerce or assist anyone else with the aforementioned activities?"

Tim hesitated. *Shit, I got him*. Adam hoped his line of questioning would lead to nothing. He counted the lieutenant as at least friendly if not a friend. This whole situation felt terrible, especially as he had to work his way through various potential suspects. Dealing with the navigator though...that in particular bothered him the most.

"I'm waiting for an answer, Lieutenant."

"I refuse to answer under article forty-seven in the New Uniform Code of Military Justice."

Adam wouldn't have been more shocked if Tim punched him in the face. He thought he might be on to something with the hesitation but a claim of silence, of invoking one of the articles...What was this boy hiding? Surely he didn't hold anyone's freedom so much higher than his own.

"I see." Adam stood and called for the security personnel who entered the room. "Place Lieutenant Collins under arrest on a charge of conspiracy to commit treason."

One of the guards took out handcuffs and bound Tim's hands. They began to lead him out of the room when Adam stopped them. He advanced, moving so he stood only a few inches from the Lieutenant, staring into his eyes. They remained silent for some time, just peering into each other's faces.

"Will you at least tell me if there were any other acts of sabotage? Are we in danger of damaging ourselves further?"

Tim hesitated again.

"Damn it, man! Your *shipmates* are on board. If something happens to them, their suffering is on *you*. Can your conscience handle that?"

"I'm not aware of any sabotage beyond the jump module, sir."

A clever answer. One that didn't incriminate himself or anyone else but it also may not be the truth. Adam stepped back and rubbed his eyes. The Uniform Code of Military Justice was quite specific as to how a member of the armed services was to be treated in the event of a criminal accusation but considering the circumstances, Adam had to wonder if an interrogator should be brought in.

One of the security people, perhaps someone Lieutenant Colonel Marshall Dupont might pick, could get the information out of the young man. But Adam didn't want to subject Tim to the indignation. Maybe someone else had the ability to talk it out of him, someone closer. Lieutenant Commander Redding seemed to get along with him and of course, there was Lieutenant Darnell.

"Take him away." Adam paced back to his desk and leaned against it as they led the young man out. He straightened his shoulders after they left and headed to the bridge. He could brief the captain in his ready room up there. The answers wouldn't make him happy, hell they made Adam miserable.

Such investigations rarely lead to a good end and this one was shaping up to be quite the tragedy.

I hope it was worth it to you, whoever masterminded this nonsense. When we find out, you're not going to be a happy camper. I promise you that.

***

Olly wiped his sweaty palms on the legs of his pants. Half the fleet stopped firing at them but the other one really laid it on heavy. He watched the shields like a hawk, ready to report on any decline in power but so far, they held strong. As they moved away, they would soon be out of range and then, he figured he'd breathe easily.

Part of his stress came from the sudden departure of Tim. He'd worked with the guy for quite a while so to have him yanked from the bridge in the middle of important action meant something really bad went down. When his replacement arrived, Ensign Leonard Marcus, he took the seat quietly and just got to work.

I guess he doesn't want to know why he got summoned here or maybe the captain told him. Either way, he looks about as freaked out as I feel.

"Ensign Marcus," Gray said. "Please double check our position and the course we have laid in to get home."

"Yes, sir."

Wow, he doesn't trust Tim's numbers. That's crazy. I guess it makes sense.

"Confirmed, sir," Leonard said. "I've matched up adjacent star maps and determined the coordinates are accurate. When we're ready to jump, we should arrive near Mars."

"Thank you," Gray replied.

Silence fell over the bridge for a moment. Olly sat up straight, eyes wide as he looked at the scanners. The fleet...they stopped firing! Their weapons went cool and their ships backed off. Any relief such an event might've provided died quickly when he saw just how close the real enemy was to getting there.

We've got twenty minutes at most. I wonder if they know about us.

Olly started running a quick program to see if they'd been scanned. He turned slightly to speak. "Captain, the fleet has stopped firing and we've got twenty minutes before the enemy ships arrive. I'm checking now to see if we've been detected."

"Looks like a little more good and bad news," Gray replied. "Let me know right away. Clea, has Raeka reached out to us yet?"

"Not yet, sir." Clea frowned. "Trying to reach them but their com channels seem to be full."

The elevator opened and Ensign Agatha White stepped into the bridge, offering a salute. Dark circles ringed her eyes but she seemed as alert as any of them. "Sorry for the delay, Captain. Ensign White reporting for duty."

"Good to have you back, Ensign." Gray motioned. "Relieve Clea from coms. She'll fill you in on what's going on."

Olly hummed. "Sir, I'm seeing some motion in the two fleets. I think they're trying to form a battle line of some kind. They might want to talk to us about the weapon capabilities first."

"First task, Ensign," Gray called out. "Get them on the horn so we can work this out. Olly, do you know if the enemy made us yet?"

"We have not been scanned by them, sir." Olly turned to Leonard. "Can you start looking for a large body? Something else like the asteroid or even a moon? Something with enough gravitational body to mask us when we reduce engine power."

"Yes, sir." Leonard started his work and Olly turned to the captain.

"Is that the plan, sir?"

"Very good, Lieutenant Darnell." Gray smirked. "I'm fairly certain the enemy isn't prepared for us. They're thinking this is another walk in the park. Let's find a position and get ready. Ensign, send a final message to those fleets and let them know if they don't answer our hails shortly, we can't coordinate. We'll be going radio silent soon."

***

Raeka paced on the bridge as the ships moved into position to take an advancing target, giving them all space to avoid a single explosion taking out multiple vessels. The tactic was shared by both cultures though they had to change it up frequently to be of any use against one another. They'd all seen it a dozen times but hopefully, it would work on the alien.

Coms were jammed but they finally got a message from the Behemoth. Gahlir flagged him down, gesturing emphatically at his station.

"They've stated they're moving off to create an ambush and have offered us some additional information. These fiends are willing to ram their enemies and their shields and weapons are on par with the Behemoth. Our weapons may not penetrate their defenses immediately. They said we're going to need to be ready to hammer them when they drop."

"So they're going to let us lure them in and spring a trap?" Raeka nodded. "Okay. But for that to be effective, we should cut our connection in case our new enemy is able to trace it. Send the other fleet this intelligence. This may be one of the biggest fights of our lives. Let's be sure to deliver it with efficiency and honor."

The rest of the bridge crew offered a resounding affirmation before diving back into their duties, coordinating all the other ships under their command. This was the kind of thing some of them lived for, a battle of overwhelming odds but the tenacity necessary to pull through. Raeka hoped that would be true this time. He'd seen rough battles before but this was an entirely different game.

One we may not even be qualified to play but that won't stop us from trying to win.

***

Wing Commander Meagan Pointer sat in her fighter wishing she could take a nap. Even with the shots the med bay handed out like candy, she felt exhausted. The adrenaline of going into battle helped a little, fending off the worst of her fatigue but the stimulants made her head ache and the back of her neck was stiff.

Stretching barely touched this nonsense. I hope being jarred around in a fighter helps. Though I don't know what I'm saying, this is going to be about as pleasant as being kicked in the face by a mule.

The rest of her wing reported in as they prepared for launch. Each of them suffered the same fatigue as her but the younger ones rubbed in a natural resistance to it. Meagan privately wondered just how much those kids drank during their time off. She considered their current condition to pretty much be a hangover.

The other wing committed to the action was a bomber squad led by Wing Commander Rudy Hale. They'd run several missions in tandem but rarely were directly together like this. The idea was they would mingle with this alien fleet, wait for the enemy to show up then harass them while the Behemoth launched an ambush attack.

Bombers were present for the moment the shields went down. Group Commander Revente told them the bridge would attempt to use Protocol Seven, a weapon which was compromised but might have limited effect on these ships. It was designed to lower the shields of the enemy, making them vulnerable to conventional attacks.

Meagan tapped into Rudy's com. "You okay over there?"

"Feel like someone hit me with a shovel but yeah, I'm fine. You?"

"Pretty close to the same."

"Nice trip, huh? On our way home then thrust into a fight out in the middle of nowhere."

"It's why I signed up," Rudy said. "Oh, here we go. Launch time. I'll see you out there."

"Just be sure your guys don't get in our way." Meagan smiled. "You guys tend to be a little slow."

"Uh huh. That's cause we actually *think* before we maneuver. Later, Pointer."

"Bye, Hale."

Each ship received clearance, bursting out of the hangar while the Behemoth continued on its path. They were moving toward a large moon, one that seemed to be orbiting a gas giant. The combination of both would cover their vessel's signature, keeping them from scans until the right moment.

As Meagan's ship launched, she hoped that time frame wouldn't be long. The fleet they encountered wouldn't last against the enemy's weapons, hell, she half believed they could take then down with three squadrons of fighters. The pulse cannons could stay on cool down. Perhaps an unkind assessment but probably an accurate one.

Leaving the ship, she took a moment to look around. Looked like every other patch of space so far. Nothing remarkable, no nebulas, none of the stuff that vids used to make it exciting. She knew it would be plenty wild soon and less peripheral distractions would be welcome.

They approached the alien vessels and her scanners documented their silhouettes, plugging them into the Friend part of her identifier. Part of the briefing spoke of their capabilities and while they might've been a match for Earth prior to alliance intervention, they were mostly relying on conventional weapons.

Their one difference came from the defensive ships they put in front of their fleet. Those supposedly erected a pretty strong shield. Calculations suggested they *might* be able to hold off a few shots and that should've been all they needed. The Behemoth would get there fast. But she remained skeptical.

As they closed in, she hailed them to establish a connection. The briefing suggested they were a bit twitchy and liked to go silent. Not the best traits for allies.

"This is Gahlir of the Emancipated Flagship," A voice translated over her speakers. "State your name and rank."

"Wing Commander Meagan Pointer. Look forward to working with you fellas. We're closing in so please don't shoot, okay?"

"We will not fire. Welcome and thank you for your assistance. We look forward to fighting at your side."

"Us too. So you've seen the briefing on these guys?"

"We're prepared."

I wish that were true.

"Good to hear!" Meagan adjusted course and maneuvered between the larger ships. The rest of her wing took position throughout the area, cutting their engines to idle. The less pulse energy they emitted, the less chance the enemy would catch on to the surprise attack. She took a deep breath and tried to settle her nerves.

They should've sent more fighters.

Apparently, two wings pushed the limit for emissions but it felt light. They had to essentially guard all these ships long enough to let them be effective. Considering how fast space combat got, she didn't have confidence they'd be able to last long enough to see them do any real damage.

Maybe I'm a naysayer…or maybe this fatigue is sapping any semblance of positivity.

"We're in position," Rudy's voice crackled in her ear. "You ready?"

"Yep." Meagan rolled her neck the best she could with her helmet on. "Can't wait, right?"

Her stomach dropped when she saw a flash on the horizon, the heat corona of the enemy on rapid approach. They'd be there in mere minutes, bringing another major battle to them. All the Behemoth pilots would walk away from their tour with more experience than most flyers would see in a lifetime.

Providing we make it back to celebrate such a claim, then it'll all be for something. God, I really am tired if I'm thinking like this. Get your head in the game, Pointer! This isn't a time for day dreaming.

Chapter 7

Clea reclaimed her position beside Gray and checked the engineering reports. As they didn't need to jump out of the system immediately, Maury took the opportunity to run some additional tests to triple check their work. A wave of relief gripped her heart as she read the positive results.

With the tuners properly aligned, leaving would no longer be a problem. Now they just had to survive the encounter with the enemy before returning home.

Clea felt torn about the decision to stay and help the people. On one hand, they would be utterly destroyed without the Behemoth's help, possibly their entire culture. Emotionally, she knew it was wrong to abandon them but rationally, she struggled. The crew still suffered from the side effects of the bad jump, the ship itself had only *just* been fully restored and many of the repairs would be hard to test properly prior to going into combat.

At least the most important elements, weapons and shields, were online but that just meant they were capable of fighting back. Successfully doing so generally required everyone to be at the top of their game. Adam's investigation didn't help much at all either. If word of it spread, morale would definitely take a hit.

The possibility of a traitor made Clea think about her sister. The alliance had their share of individuals who went against the government for one reason or another. Most of the time, they were protesting the war, pressing hard to vie for peace. None of them knew just how hard the diplomats begged for it.

The enemy simply would not listen to reason and no matter how many reports the government released or examples of their violence, a sect still remained dedicated to ending all conflict. Clea admired their tenacity but not their wisdom. They saw with their own eyes what was happening and somehow refused to believe the truth.

Those monsters out there would never stop until each and every one of them died.

Humans proved to be more pragmatic and though there were some activists, the fact that the fleet had been hit so hard in the first conflict rallied the population. The months following her joining the human crew were filled with zeal and a little xenophobia. Her commanding officer warned her it would happen but seeing it in person drove the point home.

Now, years later Clea had been accepted. Even though her sister's actions made the whole process take two steps back. She had to work twice as hard to prove her own loyalty and she was quite certain that Adam considered her to be the traitor more than once. Perhaps he still did but the fact he hadn't spoken to her yet gave her hope.

Whoever did betray them will not have a good time of it. These people hold loyalty quite high. Perhaps I should volunteer to help but then…I may be needed here. Without Adam on the bridge, I'm second in command technically. I wonder how that would play out if something happened to Gray.

"I'm putting an ETA on the screen, sir," Olly announced. "Please note the enemy will arrive in only thirteen minutes."

"A lifetime in war," Gray said. "Redding, are we ready for this?"

"Yes, sir. Engines are at full power. Weapons are charged and ready. Shields appear to be at maximum. Pilots are ready to disembark on our orders." Redding paused. "Idling at just above engine shut down. We're ready."

"Good. Let them get in here and prepare a volley and we'll dive in." Gray sighed. "I hate to use these people as bait but we'll need a little surprise on our side if we're going to make this work. Olly, you got Protocol Seven ready? Just in case it works?"

"The modified version might cause havoc with their systems," Olly replied. "And it's ready to go."

"Perfect. Here we go, ladies and gentlemen. Stay on task and we'll come out of this just fine."

Clea wanted to believe him and she saw the others shared her sentiment, though they were a bit more robust when they spoke *yes, sir*. For her part, she continued to struggle with the variables set against them. Exhaustion, recent repairs, a bunch of ships to protect and an environment they were not familiar with, all heaped on them at the same time.

If they won this fight, it would be quite the achievement and one they'd deserve some recognition for.

***

Adam went down to the brig and called in Marshall Dupont to get his ideas for interrogating Tim. The Lieutenant Colonel of security had been at the job for the better part of eighteen years. He knew the laws of the military and methods to get information out of individuals better than anyone on board and likely had a specialist at his disposal.

They gathered in the office just outside the interrogation room, speaking quietly.

"The Uniform Code of Military Justice grants him the right to silence," Adam muttered, "but we need to know who else was involved. If they try anything else, we have to stop them...right now, of all times, we need all systems operating at peak efficiency. We can't have people worrying about being stabbed in the back."

"In cases of treason," Marshall said, "we can press pretty hard for an answer but if he retains his silence, we're not legally allowed to go beyond that. He needs to cooperate to be honest."

"How do we convince him then?"

Marshall let out a breath. "Short of torturing him, which I don't think we're talking about doing, we might need a psychologist...or at least someone he trusts."

"I think he trusts Redding, but she's a little busy right now with this attack. Any other thoughts?"

"We do have a couple of shrinks on board who might get it out of him."

"That might be our best bet."

"Why don't I talk to him first?" Marshall offered. "Maybe he'll open up if I give him a view of how bad his situation is. If he knows he's looking at doing some serious time in prison, up to and including execution, he might come clean."

"I thought we did away with execution," Adam said. "People do time now, don't they? Freighter work?"

"There's an antiquated article that hasn't been revoked about field execution," Marshall said. "I'm sure a lawyer would go to town on it but for now, it does protect the *threat* at least."

"Jesus, I don't want to threaten Tim."

"We have to use whatever tools are at our disposal, Adam. If you want this information, we can't be squeamish."

"What if he turns out to be totally innocent?"

"He should've spoken up," Marshall replied. "You can't play silence without something to hide."

"Unless he doesn't believe the person he's protecting did anything."

"Damning evidence can be investigated but no evidence only leaves us one recourse." Marshall gestured toward the cells. "That young man is our only clue about what happened to this ship. You tell me: are we going to find out what he knows or hope to God he was the only one involved until we get home? Note that when we return to Earth, our culprit may well leave the ship and never come back."

"Leaving us with no suspect."

"Correct. Whoever nearly killed us all won't face any justice if we don't find them now."

"Do what you have to do...short of torture."

Marshall shook his head. "There's no protection for doing that to people and even if we did want to implement it, we couldn't do it on the ship. Everything's recorded. Believe me, this is a psychological game. Hurting the poor bastard won't do us any good."

Adam nodded. He still didn't feel good about the situation but Marshall was right. They needed to take action. As long as they weren't attempting to coerce information out of him physically, he didn't technically see anything wrong with it. He simply felt bad about the whole situation because of *who* they were interrogating.

"Do it. Whoever you need to bring in, let's get it done."

"We're on it, Commander." Marshall moved away and got on the com, contacting one of his own people.

Adam sent a report to the captain detailing out what they were about to do and letting him know that Tim looked suspicious if not flat out guilty. Gray replied back only with *understood, keep me posted*. He knew how the captain felt about the navigator so it couldn't have gone over well but then they must've been insanely busy up on the bridge.

"Did you know those invaders who attacked us showed up?" Marshall asked.

Adam nodded. "I read the report."

"I guess I had my head down in other things cause I'm the last to know. You sure we want to do this interrogation now? There seems to be bigger fish to fry."

"If we don't fight out who Tim's protecting and they screw us over during a fight, then that's going to be the biggest fish we've seen."

"Fair enough." Marshall gestured. "My interrogator's almost here. He should be able to get *something* out of our guy."

"I look forward to seeing." Marshall found a chair and peered at Tim through the one way glass. "I hope he breaks fast."

"Me too...considering the fight that's about to break out, I'd rather be coordinating that than pressing one of our own. I guess we'll see what happens."

We will at that, Adam thought. *C'mon Tim, don't make us wait.*

***

Olly tried to patiently wait for the fight but couldn't quite keep himself still. After transmitting their historical data to their new shaky allies, he received a reciprocal file from them. He had to decode but it finished while they sat near the moon, idled down for their surprise attack.

It contained some historical records of the culture's first forays into space, how they too tried to explore beyond their solar system and lost vessels. Unfortunately for them, they'd already colonized a planet and began small skirmishes back and forth. By the time they sufficiently recovered from the exploration loss, they were in the midst of a full scale war.

We still haven't figured out what happened to our own expeditionary force. I wonder what it is about leaving one's solar system. Maybe fate wants to smack down those of us not entirely ready to leave. Honestly, until we had jump technology, it wasn't entirely practical. As soon as we perfected FTL with the alliance, we traveled mostly without incident.

...well, except for this recent event of course.

But Olly did truly believe there must be *some* correlation between this new culture's tragedy and Earth's. It couldn't have been the enemy. Maybe the ships were still out there, exploring. Their own might be too, they had no way of truly knowing. Communication would eventually reach home base but if they couldn't transmit for some reason...All those years though. Survival seemed impossible.

Olly compiled the reports and sent them to the captain as low priority, for information purposes only. The ships approached, two again ready to go. Olly's passive scans weren't nearly as powerful as what he typically used but they granted him the essentials: distance to target, incoming speed and energy buildups.

Redding could use these statistics to plan her movements and fire the weapons more effectively. The captain's idea was bold but for the few seconds it would take to get into the action might be more than the fleets could handle, even with fighter support. The bombers might turn the tide. Their ordinance could be devastating.

Let's hope the wake doesn't damage our new allies. That's the last thing they need.

Olly's mind drifted to Tim and he wondered what was happening with his friend. Part of him wanted to tap into the security system and take a look at the data they were compiling but he decided against it. Any investigation they performed must've been confidential and sneaking a look would only cause more trouble.

Which is the last thing I need right now.

The captain couldn't really think Tim was capable of anything nefarious. It didn't make sense. Everyone on the bridge knew him for quite a while. He always seemed straight forward, a man who kept his comments real. He didn't flatter nor did he berate. As a team member, Olly found him to be easy to get along with.

Goes to show you may never really know someone.

***

Raeka stood beside Tarkin, reading the data on his screen. The incoming ships boasted similar power readings to the Behemoth but just different enough that they felt like they might have a chance. They calibrated the weapons for maximum power, forsaking energy efficiency for punch. Once the Behemoth got those shields down, they'd need to hit the bastards hard.

The two men worked out how the other ships in the fleet should maneuver and related the orders through Gahlir. He coordinated the various captains and expressed that many of them needed to keep in a constant state of motion. Most battles against the founders meant the scouts did most of the moving but this time, they needed to avoid weapons with the potential to annihilate them instantly.

Maybe the Behemoth should've shot one of us down after all, Raeka thought. *It would've given us some respect for what we're about to face.*

Shield ships from both sides took up position side by side and three high. Their collective shields connected and overlapped, a tactic Raeka hoped might hold back at least a few of the enemy blasts. They'd done so well in the past against each other, this defensive measure proved to be one of their strongest points.

If any of his men were nervous, he couldn't tell. They kept quiet, working hard and focusing their attention to their duties. His subordinates on the other vessels all reported in their faith in his command, reaffirming they were behind him all the way. The gesture was kind but unnecessary. He trusted them all to do their duties as well, even if it led to destruction.

We've been preparing to die for a long time.

Growing up in a state of war had an impact on the psychology of a child, a man and a soldier. As most of his friends grew from one to the next, he saw the transformation a dozen times. Death shown on the news gave them a sense of mortality long before they were ready but it toughened them up, deadened their fear.

Facing an alien was no different than the dangerous end of a Foundation missile barrage. The only difference was the things pulling the trigger didn't necessarily look like them. Even if they did, they couldn't be thought of as any more than opponents, creatures to be disposed of for the sake of survival.

What will happen if we win? How will our world change? This moment, this occasion will alter our future forever.

Raeka hoped for the best but felt they would be entering a new phase of conflict, one with outside forces instead of internal ones. For the first time in generations, the Founders and Emancipated would unite again. Perhaps it would last, allowing them to become one country, healing the schism keeping them apart.

The Earth fighters kept in contact, letting them know their relative position to their various ships. They were tiny barbs scattered amongst the grass, a tactic Raeka approved of. Captain Atwell proved to have a tactical mind, which didn't seem likely the way they avoided fighting them earlier.

The ability to not *attack may well prove the courage of a man over striking an opponent any day.*

Tarkin certainly was impressed and relieved as well. Had the Behemoth opened up on them, many people would've died. Raeka would never have forgiven himself for pushing the Earth ship to such an extreme. They experienced some pretty blind luck when the ship destroyed an asteroid instead of a cruiser or destroyer.

"Sir, two minutes to contact," Gahlir called. "The fight's about to begin."

Here we go. Raeka took a deep breath and returned to his seat. Now was the moment of truth when they would face off against an overwhelming opponent. For good or ill, this would determine the fate of them all. Such a responsibility may not have been easy to carry but Raeka had been doing it for some time.

***

Major Harrington Bean took a quick briefing from Lieutenant Colonel Dupont about the situation with Timothy Collins. Interrogation in the midst of combat seemed insane but the orders were very clear. The problem came at whether or not he could be effective knowing what was going on outside. A major battle might well distract him from some of his best techniques.

Harrington worked in security for a long time and spoke to many criminals. He'd pulled confessions out of men who clung to innocence on several occasions but never on board a ship, never a bridge officer and certainly not while being shot at. Of course, Commander Everly was involved and seemed to think it was all okay so he tried to mentally calm down before heading down to the brig.

Once there, Harrington found the young man sitting at a table with his hands bound on top, cuffed to the table itself. *They really think this kid's involved in the treason if they've done that. We only bind violent criminals down like that. This is intense.*

Tim didn't look up when he entered and continued to stare at the surface of the table, barely moving other than to breathe. Harrington pulled out the chair opposite him and sat down, wondering what techniques he'd have the chance to employ before things got crazy. The fact is, he would normally let the suspect sweat a while but they apparently didn't have the luxury.

Get it out of him as quickly as you can, Harry, Marshall said. *We're counting on you...this could mean life or death for a lot of people.*

Thanks, Lieutenant Colonel. No pressure at all. Harrington drew another breath and leaned forward. "Good afternoon, Lieutenant."

"I doubt I'll have that rank much longer, sir."

Harrington shrugged. "I suppose that depends on what you did, or did not do, right?"

"I'm afraid I'm invoking my right to silence under article forty-seven in the New Uniform Code of Military Justice."

"Yeah, I heard you pulled that one out," Harrington said. "Who put you up to that?"

Tim remained silent.

"You can talk about other things...let's chat about how you got your commission."

Tim looked at him. "What do you mean?"

"Can you talk to me about your endorsement?"

"Admiral Jameson gave it to me."

Harrington nodded. "He must've really seen something in you...a lot of potential."

"I suppose so."

"How do you think he'd feel about you right now? Knowing you've been arrested on treason charges."

Tim looked away but didn't speak.

"Do you think he'd be disappointed? Maybe even upset?"

"Admiral Jameson has *many* opinions, sir...and passions."

"You'd know. You worked as one of his aides, right?"

"A junior," Tim nodded, "yes, sir."

"Did you like it?"

Tim paused. "It was okay, sir."

"Just okay? Big duty for someone *just* out of the academy. From cadet to ensign working for an admiral. Huge role for a kid."

"I did research for them and was on a whole team. I'd say we had over ten people...maybe more."

Harrington hummed. "Anyone else from that team aboard this ship?"

"No, sir. They pursued planet side duties. None of them had the astrogation background I did."

"You always wanted to take to the stars."

"Yes, sir."

"Let's cut the shit for a minute, Tim. You're on the line here. You have the know how and skill to do what you're being accused of. We can make these charges stick and even if you're not the right person, you might end up taking the fall. Why throw your career and life away? Confide in me. Tell me who you're backing up so we can end this with a reprimand."

Tim's brows lifted. "You think I'm stupid enough to think after all this I'd get a verbal?"

"Loyalty's important but blindly giving it can be dangerous. Think about it. Backing up your crew is an essential part of our success as officers but there does come a time when you have to cash that in. I know you care about what happens to you. You've spent too much time getting good at your job, learning what you did and studying. Your passion for the stars will go to waste in a cell."

"Treason can lead to a death sentence," Tim said. "Can't it?"

Harrington shrugged. "Not as much anymore. You'd have to do a lot worse than *nearly* destroying the ship. There's plenty of room in prison these days, especially mining operations. They always need an extra set of hands and a strong back. You've got both, least for a while. Consider my point: there are worse things than dying and believe me, command *will* use them."

"And I'm to believe you're my buddy." Tim tilted his head, scowling.

"Not at all. I'm the guy who they sent in here to get information. You know that. I'm also the guy who can authorize you to leave. If you want to be friends, I'm game but the honest truth is I'm more interested in finding the person you're hiding. I want to get home and I'd like to think you're interested in the same thing."

"What's going to happen to them?"

"At least you've actually just admitted there is a *them*." Harrington pointed out. "And they'll be arrested and questioned, of course. What do you think we're doing here, Collins? Planning a surprise birthday party? We're talking about high stakes here. Lives are on the line and you're futzing around with them."

"I..." Tim shook his head. "I have to think about it."

"You don't have long, my friend so think fast. Before long, those guys waiting in the hall are going to get pissed and when they do, they'll open the playing field up. Right now, we're just talking. They bring medical into the game...we're talking shots and heavier interrogation techniques but I'm *convinced* you'd rather do the right thing."

"I'm trying to determine what exactly that is."

"Hardest question a man can ever ask himself," Harrington said. "And believe me, I ask questions all the time. But this isn't one you should be stuck on. You've been around long enough to know what all this means. You've read the history books of how badly a mole can damage the infrastructure of a military unit."

"I know, sir...but..."

"We're getting somewhere. You want to tell me. Just come out with it. No one's judging you. Unless you have direct involvement in this action, you don't have anything to worry about. Did you?"

Tim looked up at him sharply and shook his head. "I...have to maintain my silence...on the uniform—"

"Yes, I know the schtick," Harrington interrupted. "That silence shit isn't going to protect either of you. Or if there are more, I'd like to know that too. Are we talking a team? Or just you and one more? What did you do for them? Did they just tell you about it? Come on, Lieutenant. We were so close to a revelation there."

"I think we've got worse problems right now, sir." Tim straightened his shoulders. "And if it's all the same to you, I'd like to wait to answer these questions until after the engagement has ended...so I know whether or not I need to do this."

"You've already betrayed everyone who trusted you aboard this ship," Harrington said, standing up. "What's stopping you from betraying those who wanted to destroy it?"

"That wasn't the point..." Tim snapped his mouth shut and looked away. Harrington smirked.

"I see."

"Please don't take that..."

"What?" Harrington feigned an innocent expression. "Don't waste my time with trying to cover up your slip. You gave me some valuable information right now. Think about it for a few minutes. I'll be back in five and believe me, if I leave again, any chances or deals will go with me. So really think. How do you want to be remembered, Lieutenant Collins?"

"I don't think I've got a choice now, do I?"

"We all have choices unless we're dead. Second chances end then. You've got one right now. Time to make good on it, don't you think?" Harrington stepped to the door. "Talk to you in a little while. Make sure you focus on self preservation while I'm gone. I think you need a healthy dose of it."

Chapter 8

Meagan's fatigue drained away as the enemy approached. Her scanners picked them up, two massive ships coming in hot. She watched the kilometers drop rapidly from the hundreds of thousands to the tens of thousands. Then, they were on them, pulse blasts lighting up the darkness of space without a moment's hesitation.

No hails, no warnings. Just like them to be consistent.

Surprisingly, their ally's shields held from the first barrage but the energy output was enormous. They turned bright orange with every hit and lights all over the ships dimmed with every impact. Meagan counted to five, giving the enemy a moment to register what was happening before squeezing her flight stick.

"That's our cue, Panther," she called out to the two wings. "Let's make this happen. Bear One, you guys take the flank. We'll draw their fire."

"You've just got to be a hero," Rudy replied. "Good luck, Panther One."

Meagan's ship vibrated for a moment as she engaged full throttle, pulling away from the vessels around her. The rest of her wing formed up with her, building velocity. The inertial dampeners moaned when she pulled up, changing direction fast enough to kill a pilot without the safety technology in place.

Squadron Leader Mick Tauran moved along side her as they rocketed forward, their hulls shimmering with their own shields in place. The moment any of them fired, the enemy would likely deploy their own fighters. Then, if the Behemoth didn't get there in time, Panther and Bear would be outnumbered by a lot.

They'd proven to have superior tactics in the past but this situation was different. They had no technological equals supporting them. The last engagement with the enemy involved a lot of alliance ships and before that, they had high tech drones providing some cover. This time, it was all them and some low tech ships with enough defenses to survive an initial assault.

Impressive but not exactly confidence boosting.

Meagan led her ships down from their allies then out away from the shields. Once they cleared them, they climbed and moved along side the enemy. All the pulse turrets blasted at the fleet and hadn't taken notice of the bees about to sting them. Meagan initiated the clearance to attack, a poke with their own pulse technology to show they weren't up against total schlubs.

Spinning her ship to the side, Meagan took the lead for the first attack run, strafing the top of their enemy with several blasts before pulling up and performing evasive maneuvers. The smooth surface of her target filled her view for several moments and her cockpit warmed up every time she pulled the trigger.

As she yanked back on the stick, blackness spread out before her, distant stars doing little to break up the curtain of space. She moved erratically, making it difficult to get a lock on her as she bought distance. The others of her wing did the same, dancing fireflies above a dangerous foe intent on killing everything in its path.

"You on it, Bear?" Mick called out the question, filling every radio in their two wings.

"Right now, Panther," Rudy replied. "Keep your trousers on but stay back. These bombs aren't going to be pretty."

Meagan checked her scans, ensuring all her people made it far enough away to avoid the shockwave. Minimum safe distance was only a few hundred kilometers away and they passed it easily. The ships around her loosened their formation and turned just in time to witness Bear squadron let loose an impressive volley of missiles, enough to devastate a small moon.

Each projectile hammered the shields of the first enemy capital ship, causing a dramatic blue-purple flare of energy to dance in every direction. The bombers raced away from the shockwave, getting behind their new ally's shields in time to avoid being caught up in it. The enemy shields held but they fulfilled Meagan's prediction and launched fighters of their own.

"Time to engage," Meagan called out. "They're going to slow down with those turrets now to give their ships a chance to take us out."

As they paired up, she took a moment to check the scans again, zeroing in on the Behemoth's relative location. They were racing into the battle, about to batter the enemy's flank. Fighter reinforcements would be there soon as well, swaying the odds back to something manageable.

The computer gave them an ETA of two minutes.

We have to survive a hundred and twenty seconds out here...shouldn't be too bad. Just harass and keep moving.

The first group of fighters raced toward them and they spread out, giving them more targets to chase. Earth's pilots learned early on that the enemy tended to go at them one at a time, choosing an erratic and chaotic tactic over supporting one another. This gave the Behemoth fliers a small advantage in that someone always had their back.

As one in particular tried to tack onto Meagan's six, Mick hit the breaks and took up position behind the attacker. Meagan moved with practiced ease, luring her pursuer into a perfect trap which allowed Mick an easy shot, a flurry of pulse fire tearing up the fuselage of his target.

The explosion behind her still lit up her cockpit and Mick sounded off, splash one. *An anachronistic term but it still works*.

Other ships moved in, flying in wild, evasive circles. They unleashed random cannon fire at their targets, making the attacks difficult to avoid. Meagan and Mick spread out to the sides and flanked two, catching them in a crossfire as they tried to spin out of the way. Both ships exploded and the Panther fighters flew over the cascading debris, their shields flaring up from contact with particles of metal.

Meagan's computer buzzed, indicating one of their own fighters had been hit. She was too busy to see who but did a call out for Roll Call while dedicating the rest of her attention to dodging incoming attacks. Panther Five didn't report in, Lieutenant Leslie Eddings. *I hope you bailed out okay…* The others were still in the fight.

Rudy's wing managed a second attack run but they didn't seem to fare well as they tried to rocket away. At least two of them took hits but Meagan had no idea if the ships were destroyed, damaged or unscathed. Her own computer remained attached only to her people, anything more would be overwhelming in a large scale assault.

The enemy ships kept coming, waves of them pouring out of the two capital ships. Meagan forced herself to focus on the task directly at hand, ignoring the odds stacking ever higher against them. If the Behemoth didn't arrive soon with reinforcements...*Stop thinking. Work. You've got to hold this for as long as it takes. You can do it.*

Another five fighters moved in, trying to get on her tail. *Not exactly instilling me with confidence here.* She pulled up on the stick and prepared to engage, steadying herself for what might be the inevitable.

***

Raeka watched the Behemoth fighters dash into battle without any regard for their own safety, throwing their lives on the line for people they'd never even met. Their honor shamed him for attacking their ship and he desperately wanted to do something to help them. He maintained discipline, however, and focused on holding the line. The Behemoth gave strict tactics to handle the invaders.

If we want to survive this, we have to defer to experience. The power of these vessels!

When the enemy started pounding their shields, the power output went off their scale. He didn't even know how their defenses held but felt proud they did. It became quite obvious their weapons would not hurt these things though and if the Behemoth fighters hadn't been there, a quick flanking run would remove their only chance to hold them at all.

"The Behemoth is on the move," Gahlir called out. "They'll be here momentarily."

"None too soon," Raeka said. "These fighters need support...support we cannot provide."

"When those shields go down..." Tarkin grumbled. "Ours, or there's, this battle will be over quickly."

"Maybe not," Gahlir said. "Their hulls are armored...I still can't tell what they are. Our scans won't penetrate their defenses."

"It won't matter," Raeka replied. "Combining our power with the Behemoth, we'll overwhelm them. I have to believe that."

Optimism at a time like this is difficult but what's the alternative?

***

Gray leaned forward, willing himself to not tap his foot. Redding pushed them to full throttle, coming up fast on the enemy's flank. Fighter crews were standing by to launch the moment they got within range. Less than two minutes and they'd be in the fight, assaulting their foes. He hoped it would be at least a fraction of a surprise.

Even a moment of shock will take us a long way.

"Bad news," Olly said. "I've run a scan and the Protocol Seven will *not* work on these guys. They must've been updated. I am jamming their communications, however. They won't be telling anyone about us any time soon."

"That proliferated fast," Clea said. "I…honestly can't even believe it."

"I'm not surprised," Gray replied. "These bastards seem geared for one thing: conflict. If that's the case, the first thing I'd do is share the cure to a weapon our entire fleet. It was a chance, but one we don't get to rely on. Thanks, Olly. Anything else?"

"Yes, sir. Fighters engaged," Olly said. "Bombers have conducted their first run."

"Any appreciable damage?" Clea asked.

"Negative, Ma'am. The shields held...though power output suggests they *did* tax them."

"Incredible." Gray shook his head. "Those bombs can devastate moons, for God's sake."

Clea showed him her computer, indicating they seemed to be doubling their defenses. He frowned at the figures on the screen. How had they known to do so? Perhaps they scanned the incoming vessels and decided to do it. The act made them slow down with the turrets which bought the Emancipated and Founder fleets time.

I guess it worked out for the best.

Gray checked his own reports. All sections of the ship reported in, displaying positive reports of all systems remaining operational. *Thank God for that. At least we don't have anything breaking down as we push into a fight. Of course, the real test will come when we start firing our weapons...and more importantly, when we're hit back.*

Engineering stated that the jump module likely could *not* stand up to microjumping but Gray had no intention of attempting another such maneuver before the engineers back home could really delve into the issues they experienced from them before. They could, however, flee at any time, a comment made by Maury in his quick update.

We're not abandoning these people, Gray thought. He sent back a message thanking the Chief Engineer for his assessment. *He's one of the few people who knows about the traitor. That must be where he's coming from. If we don't know who's causing trouble, he feels we should've left the system to find out.*

Prudence made sense. However, just because the objective of the fight didn't coincide with direct Earth plans didn't mean it was unnecessary. A skirmish outside the confines of their own territory just meant they were at war and two less enemy ships were fewer vessels to attack alliance or Sol space.

Targets of opportunity. These guys can't get back home.

"We're approaching optimal range for a firing solution," Redding announced. "On your command, I'll open fire."

"Olly," Gray said, "can the fighters launch?"

"Aye, sir. They could be in the fight within thirty seconds."

"Redding, open fire," Gray ordered. "When we're on recharge, get the fighters out there. Coordinate to make sure they're well away before we're ready to fire again."

Both acknowledged and Gray turned his attention to the screen. Their cannons fired, blasting the side of the enemy vessel with all the force they could muster. Shields flared and flickered out and a globe of fire burst from the hull. It didn't destroy them, not by a long shot, but it did do some damage.

Perfect.

Olly gave the order for the fighters to launch.

Gray tapped his communication console and raised Raeka on the line. "Open fire on the ship we just hit. Give them everything you've got and don't let up until you find yourselves hitting shield again."

The Emancipated fleet didn't even respond before firing their weapons. Conventional ordinance hammered the Enemy vessel, decorating the hull with tiny pockmarks of fire and crumpled metal. They were able to fire for nearly fifteen seconds before the shields sprung back to life, preventing further damage.

"How'd they bring their shields back?" Leonard asked. "We hit them hard!"

"They have tertiary generators," Clea said. "When one goes down, the others kick back on. We have a variable window to hurt them when that happens, anywhere from ten seconds to a full minute."

"We got screwed then," Leonard muttered the last part.

"Stow the commentary," Gray ordered. "Are they focusing on us yet, Olly?"

"Not yet, sir." Olly really scrutinized his screen for a moment. "They seem to be redoubling their efforts on the two fleets…they want to take that shield down."

"Why?" Redding asked. "And we're at sixty percent recharge on weapons."

Clea hummed. "Perhaps they realize that if they take out the natives, we'll have no reason to be here. They must know we don't belong."

"Won't matter for long," Gray said. "Redding, fire at will. When the main cannons are back, hit them again. We'll keep at them until they take notice or are destroyed."

"What if they try to flee?" Clea asked. "Do you propose we give chase?"

Gray sighed. "We can't let them get away…not with the news of our arrival and how ineffective the native's technology is. They'll be back and take this place guaranteed."

"Then I hope we can cripple them quickly."

Besides, Gray thought, *I don't think these guys know how to retreat…or surrender for that matter.*

***

Meagan initiated a spinning barrel roll, disengaging from a group of enemy fighters. Mike tore in behind them, firing off pulse blasts into the group following her. At least one exploded but she was too busy maintaining control of her ship to check the scans. The computer indicated she'd taken a grazing hit to one of the thrusters on the left. It would hamper her maneuverability eventually but for the moment, all systems operated normally.

"We've got four more incoming!" Panther Seven shouted. "You got my back?"

Panther Eight replied in the affirmative. *We're all tapped out,* Meagan thought. *C'mon, Behemoth!*

Another shot splashed against her shield, knocking her to the left so hard the inertial dampeners whined as they tried to compensate. She tensed up as the edges of her vision darkened for a moment. When she fully recovered her senses, she pressed the stick forward, disengaging to get a better position.

"Trying to catch you up," Mick shouted. "You okay, Meagan?"

"Took a shot," she replied. "Not sure how bad. Diagnostics are running slow."

"I'm running a scan...whoa!" Meagan turned to look in time to see Mick nearly take a full barrage from two different attackers. His shields flared but held and he pulled away, performing a wild maneuver. He climbed, spun and came around to unleash his own attack. He dusted two of them and the other tried to pull away.

Meagan took the opportunity to move in behind the last of them and fired, tearing through its shields then popping the hull.

"You're out of control," Meagan said to Mick. "Amazing flying."

"Thanks...glad to impress but we're not exactly coming out of this unscathed."

"Shit." Mick sighed. "Check your eleven o'clock."

Meagan's stomach sunk as she looked at her scanner. Another five ships came at them, coming in hot. The rest of Panther wing were spread throughout the area, engaged in their own conflicts throughout the combat zone. She checked her diagnostic while she had the chance. She was losing power from the earlier damage.

The read out told her *estimated time to engine depletion, five minutes*.

That's quick, Meagan thought. *Great. Well...we can at least take these guys before I'm out of the fight.*

She sent the report over to Mick's ship. "We have a problem."

It took him a moment to reply. When he finally did, he cleared his throat, "then let's give them hell before you've got to sit this out."

"Looking forward to it," Meagan replied.

They altered course, heading straight at the enemy. *I guess it's time for some chicken.* Meagan tilted her head, taking a deep breath as she focused on what might well be their final few minutes. She hit the targeting computer, letting it zero in on the nearest of the enemy ships. Mick pinged the one on the left.

Who am I kidding? When those things start shooting, we're both done.

Scans indicated the enemy was nearly within optimal range to fire….

…when one of the approaching fighters exploded.

"What the hell?" Mick looked up. "Whoa, look at friend or foe!"

Meagan risked a glance and felt a surge of relief. Three more wings from the Behemoth joined the fray, tearing through the hordes of enemy fighters. Explosions erupted all around them, purple-red globes of fire that winked out into nothingness moments later. Off to the left, the capital ships engaged, pulse blasts igniting the darkness of space.

"Panther One, this is Cheetah One. Hope you don't mind the hand. You guys looked like you had this under control."

"Yeah, we were good," Meagan joked. "We're all pretty banged up out here, Cheetah One. We're going to disengage and RTB for repair and reload."

"Roger that. We'll take it from here."

Meagan gave the order to the rest of her wing to haul ass back to the Behemoth. They made it, surviving some pretty overwhelming odds to buy some time and keep their allies alive throughout. As they started away, she checked her diagnostics again, noting she'd just *barely* make it back to the ship before running out of power.

Cutting it close. She let out a breath and sent a message to Rudy. "How're you guys doing?"

"Lost one," Rudy replied. "The rest of us are behind those shields waiting for our chance to bomb the hell out of the enemy again."

"Good luck, we took a lot of damage out there so we're heading back." Meagan paused. "We're going to need search and rescue for Panther Five."

"We need it too," Rudy replied. "I'm on it, Meagan. Just get back to base. I expect to talk to you later."

"No problem buddy. Be safe until we get back."

Meagan knew the chances of Panther getting back into the fight were slim to none. Considering how long it would take to get the ships back in order, the battle may be over. One way or another, they'd either win or be dead. *Ah, that pessimism again. Considering what we just pulled off, I can't believe I'm not all patriotic zeal. Maybe it's returning with a busted up ship.*

Never makes me feel particularly optimistic.

***

"All wings have engaged the enemy," Olly announced.

"Weapons are recharged," Redding added. "Firing at will."

Gray listened to the reports and for the first time since he woke up from the jump event, he felt like things were returning to normal. His confidence lifted and he considered the situation they were in tenable. Not even a month ago, this fight would've intimidated him and with his ship in the state it was, victory might've been beyond reckoning.

Now, it felt like just another engagement, only made challenging by the introduction of the new culture and the possibility of a traitor. He knew no fight would ever go by as a totally routine affair. There would always be complications but that was all part of being in the military. Overcoming odds was the most important part of his job description.

Tim weighed on his conscience. Gray held him in high regard, considered him a fantastic officer and would've thought him beyond reproach. After reading Adam's brief reports, he felt like something of a fool. How could he have been so blind? He only hoped that the decision to betray the Behemoth came recently...though there were no good reasons to do so.

And no excuses. Whether Tim directly betrayed them or was protecting someone who did, he would be prosecuted to the fullest extent of the law. Gray wanted to hold out hope that he might prove to be innocent, that there would be a solid explanation exonerating the young officer but the chances were ridiculously slim.

"Message from the Emancipated captain," Agatha said. "Their shields are overloading. They've had one reactor meltdown. Their technicians estimate they can only maintain their defense for another ten minutes at the current rate of enemy fire."

"Great. We need to push hard. Let's get multiple bomber wings on that one ship and see if we can take them out of the equation. I'm sure we can get the other ship's attention then."

"I'm on it, sir," Redding said. "Permission to close on the enemy."

"Permission granted. Get in their face if you have to." Gray turned to Agatha. "Tell our new allies to get moving. Spread out to make fewer targets and get ready to hit them hard when we send the word. If all goes according to plan, they can spend some time licking their wounds while we take on the other ship on our own."

"Panther wing has just boarded," Olly said. "They sustained some pretty heavy damage and lost one fighter."

Gray sighed. "Understood. Get a report ASAP and see what needs to happen to make them combat ready again."

"Tech teams are on it."

Clea turned to him. "Looking over the readings of the Emancipated fleet's damage, I think we may want to recommend they create some distance from their ship that lost the reactor. If it blows, I estimate considerable collateral damage."

"Relay that," Gray said. "Though I suspect they know."

"Looking at their tactics, I'm not so sure." Clea frowned. "There's another reason they'll want to move. The enemy is going to realize they have formidable defenses soon and once they do, they'll change up their tactics. I think you know what that means."

"They'll ram them?"

"And won't even take any appreciable damage in the act."

Gray nodded. "Let them know that too. I'm starting to get offended that we're being ignored. I'm hoping we make it pretty clear to them they're making a big mistake."

Redding fired the weapons, making the hull vibrate for a brief moment. The volley hammered the starboard side of their target, blasting into the shields. They shimmered from the contact and suddenly, the vessel began to turn, their engines firing up to move on the Behemoth.

"Here we go," Gray muttered. "Get the bombers in position…when those shields drop, let's devastate them fast. Don't let up on them, Redding. Give them everything we've got with as much evasive as you can manage."

"Which basically means keep different shield sections to port," Redding replied. "I'm on it, sir."

"We gained control with our sneak attack," Gray said. "Let's push our advantage and finish it up, folks. There's a lot riding on our choices. I don't intend to let any of them down."

***

Raeka gripped his seat tightly as their ship rocked from a nearby explosion. One of their ships lost their reactor and blew. The shields held but only barely. Engineering staff worked overtime, trying to keep their equipment cool enough to maintain for another few moments. Luckily, the enemy ship had to recharge so they could not maintain continuous fire.

If they had that ability, we'd all be dead.

They already lost quite a few people, at least eight ships in total on both sides. Many may have escaped, depending on how fast the crews got to the life boats but Raeka knew they would hear about a large number of dead when the fighting ended. Their own weapons did nothing against the enemy shields but just like when they attacked the Behemoth, it didn't stop them from trying.

One never knew when the enemy might lose their defenses and become vulnerable.

The enemy fighters also harassed them quite effectively but the Earth fighters did a good job of driving them off. Fortunately, those smaller ships *were* effected by the Emancipated fleet's weapons and though they were hard to hit, they did take a few out here and there. They adjusted their thinking, converting to antiaircraft tactics, which they rarely needed to bother with.

They didn't employ fighters as these two cultures did.

Maybe we should consider it. No matter how this turns out, we're going to have to deal with these aliens again. This is only the beginning of a much longer engagement. Anyone who thinks otherwise, is a fool.

Raeka mentally prepared some of his report, taking in the tactics of both the enemy and their new allies alike. Watching the way they maneuvered to keep shield sections out of the line of fire, giving the enemies new targets made sense to him. Their fighters were a devastating part of the battle and frankly kept the Emancipated and Founder fleets alive. Their distraction tactics were nasty, especially since they were capable of hurting their targets.

An interesting way to fight wars. With such destructive and defensive technologies at their disposal, it makes sense that they would have to be creative with how they got around their disadvantages. I applaud them, even as I shudder to think what might come next in the evolution of conflict.

Raeka received another update about a reactor overload. He had them relay the information to the Behemoth so they could understand their situation. No one expected them to disengage to save them, but the information would come in handy. If for some reason the two fleets went down, after all, the Behemoth would be required to face both vessels entirely alone.

At least we're providing them a distraction. For now. That's all we can ask for. Buy some time...and stay alive.

Chapter 9

Harrington waited in the hallway while Tim had a chance to think about his situation. Adam and Marshall stood nearby, doing their best to remain quiet but he could tell it wasn't easy for them. They wanted results but needed to be patient. Even if they could do *anything* to the Lieutenant, he wouldn't give up his secrets instantly.

Adam couldn't help himself and finally stepped forward. "May I remind you of what's at stake here?"

"Of course, sir." Harrington nodded. "But I know my job. If we want the *truth*, we have to be patient and get it the right way."

"Commander," Marshall pulled him aside, "let me talk to you about this over here."

They left Harrington alone and he turned his attention back to Tim. The ship began to vibrate for a moment as the engines engaged. Another tremor made him touch the wall, though it wasn't quite bad enough to put him off balance. *That was a hit. Okay, so the fighting's real. I get it guys. You don't have to convince me I need to hurry.*

Another tactic came to mind, one which catered to their urgency. He entered the interrogation room again, this time slamming the door behind him. Tim looked up with wide eyes and when Harrington slapped the table, he jumped.

"I'm sure you just felt those two tremors and you know what they mean. Right now, you have an opportunity to come clean while it matters. I'm going to give you a new piece of the deal. If you don't fess up before the fighting's done, I'll ensure you do the maximum sentence for aiding and abetting."

"I...what..."

"If you're curious, the sentence will depend on what the person you're protecting did. It could mean execution."

"You're not serious!"

"I'm dead serious, Collins. This is getting stupid. You're not a petulant child waiting to be scolded for skipping class in primary. As an officer in the military, you have expectations you're not living up to. One of them involves conducting yourself with honor. Right now, your silence isn't doing anyone any favors."

"Maybe I need to take the consequences for this."

"So you considered your self preservation and came up with this? That you want to go down for someone else? Know that they're going to get caught, Collins. It's just a matter of time." The ship shook again. "Another shot. Come clean, Lieutenant. This is your last chance because when I walk out that door this time, I'm going to help *real* soldiers in this fight and you can rot."

Tim clenched his fists, his expression full of torment. Harrington started to count. When he reached ten, he'd walk. The lieutenant had that much time to make a decision and save himself from the worst penalty his crime might warrant. Either that or the Commander would come in and beat the hell out of him, stick him with needles...any of that was out of Harrington's purview.

Anything an interrogator got without a conversation should be considered suspect anyway. A man would do anything to stop a beating and drugs weren't reliable. Confessions under the influence of most narcotics didn't hold up in court. Harrington saw many cases overturned when doctors testified to the inefficiency of injections.

However, to get some quick information, he recognized their usefulness.

Harrington reached nine and turned to leave when Tim spoke up. "Wait! Sir...wait..."

"Make it fast, Lieutenant. Wasting my time right now won't endure you to me. I've got no more patience."

"They said they only wanted to show an inefficiency...something to stir up trouble between the alliance and Earth."

"Okay, you want to talk motive first, you can but if you don't have names at the end..." Harrington let the threat hang there, not bothering to tell him specifically what might happen. In cases like this, imagination worked far better than actual threats. "Go."

"The order came just before we left the mining facility. A coded message to a select few people."

"Really. How did that get covered up? All incoming communications are monitored and recorded."

"The on duty com officer took care of that," Tim muttered. "Ensign Amos Roper."

"That's one name." Harrington tapped it into his tablet. "So he deleted the message?"

"After copying it, yes, sir. He brought the information to Lieutenant Conway. She shared it with both of us but I...I didn't want anything to do with it."

"Are you saying you didn't help them?"

Tim hesitated but finally shook his head. "No, sir. I can't say that. I helped..."

Harrington sighed. "Okay, so you've admitted to helping saboteurs mess with the jump module. Explain to me how each of you took down security to make it happen."

"Lieutenant Conway didn't have clearance for the engine room but Amos had the computer knowhow to get past that. She altered the security feeds and gave herself someone else's clearance, Clea An'Tufal."

"Is it sufficient to say you were hoping to set her up?"

"Yes, sir. That was part of the plan but Commander Everly didn't seem to believe it when he conducted his investigation. I think he wanted to...but the evidence was thin. I told them that too. I mentioned any attack on Clea would probably not work. She had plenty of opportunities to cause trouble and never did. Why now? No answer would be sufficient, especially for the captain."

"I'm going to keep my curiosity to myself on that last part," Harrington muttered. "So Conway screwed with security and gained access. What part of this master plan did you have to do with?"

"I provided her an alibi. I didn't know it at the time but three weeks ago, when she invited me to stay with her...I just thought we were getting together. I always thought she was attractive. She had plans, of course...and they came from a reputable source but she didn't tell me until we were already seeing each other for a week."

"Not exactly a long time to convince someone to commit treason."

"The orders, sir..." Tim clenched his fists again. "They came from...from Admiral Jameson."

"I hope you idiots kept those orders."

"I made a copy, sir. Lieutenant Conway doesn't know."

Harrington smirked. "You might've just saved yourself from a death sentence. Naturally, you're going to have to testify against Conway and Roper. Are you prepared for that?"

"Yes, sir." Tim looked down. "I hated what we did...but I wasn't going to come forward."

"One of your many mistakes." Harrington moved to the door. "I'm going to report this and you'll be moved back to the brig. Good luck, son. I'm afraid you're going to need it."

***

The first enemy blast shook the ship but the shields held. Gray narrowed his eyes as Redding unleashed another attack of their own. Out there somewhere, fighters engaged in a life and death struggle even as the bombers got into position to help them take down this foe in one of their first toe to toe battles.

Luckily, the other ship seemed occupied trying to take on the other fleets. They maintained their defenses, even as they tried to withdraw but it was only a matter of time before they went down. Gray turned to Clea. "Do you think there's anything you and Olly can suggest to those folks about recalibrating their power and protecting themselves for a little longer?"

"I doubt it, sir," Olly answered. "Their technology, while less potent than ours, isn't close enough to the way we do things to offer much in the way of ideas. We might well cause more harm than good."

"It's worth looking into," Clea added. "We're on it, sir."

"Thank you." Gray turned to his own computer and read a report from Adam. The words made his heart sink and his stomach ache.

Lieutenant Collins confessed. His co-conspirators were Lieutenant Theresa Conway and Ensign Amos Roper. It seems they were all operating under Admiral Jameson's orders. The goal was to frame Clea for the event. We're taking the other two into custody shortly and will stow them in the brig.

Gray rubbed his eyes. *God damn it, Tim! You had a bright future, kid! Why did you throw it all away? They are* not *going to go easy on you, even with your confession! You're done!*

Clea gently touched his forearm. "Captain, are you okay?"

He turned to her and nodded. "I'm fine, Clea. Sorry, the fatigue..."

"And whatever you just read," Clea finished for him. She nodded. "Understood, sir. When and if you need to speak about it, do let me know...after the fight of course."

Gray managed a thin smile. "Indeed. Let's get focused on the task at hand." He wrote a message back to Adam, a simple one word comment. *Understood*.

A hint of rage tickled his heart, anger at his officer for betraying them. He decided to take it out on the enemy, to focus on them and consider all the possible ways to end the fight quickly. They already had a good plan for the first one. The trick came from who would take down the other's shields first.

I've got an idea. Gray got Group Commander Estaban Revente on the line. "I need you to consider something. What do you say to coordinated bombing runs to tear down their shields? Swarm them with waves of ordinance?"

"We can make it happen, sir. I trust you want to coordinate with Redding as she fires the pulse cannons?"

"You've got it. You'll need to get some escorts for them though. As soon as the first wave hits, they're going to focus their attention on the bombers and try to take them out."

"Understood. I've got the crew for the job. I'll have the wing commanders link up with Redding. Revente out."

Gray leaned back and took a deep breath. If this tactic worked, they'd be able to chew through the enemy vessel. He anticipated the other one would flee or at least start moving to make themselves a much more difficult target. At that point, they'd pursue and the fighting would be mostly on them.

I'm sure I'll come up with something else by then though. For now, one battle at a time.

***

Rudy received the orders to take his wing out of waiting and prepare for a bombing run. Each bomber wing was expected to coordinate with the bridge, firing their bombs at the right time to ensure pulse turrets connected close to the same time as their attacks. He understood the idea but after the second wing fired, the rest would be in serious jeopardy.

I wish Meagan were out here right now.

"Who'll be our escorts?" Rudy asked. "And when will they be here?"

"You're going to have to trust me," Revente said. "I'll have the fighters there but you won't see them until the enemy sends theirs against you. Then I'll have ours engage. Hopefully, that'll limit the number they send. I'm guessing they figure you guys are sitting ducks against their faster vessels."

"We are," Rudy replied. "Make no doubt about it, this is a dangerous plan."

"I thought you liked dangerous stuff, Rudy," Revente said. "This is the kind of mission heroes are born from."

"Or die in," Rudy muttered. "But I trust you, sir. We've got the armor and shields to take a few blows. Don't worry about us."

"Alright, I'm sending everyone out there your place in line and when you'll do your first strike. We don't stop until you run out of ordinance or that thing blows up. And guys? Be sure to get out of range before any major shockwave takes you. I don't want search and rescue looking for you because you got caught up in an explosion."

"Understood." Several voices joined Rudy as the other wings prepared themselves for the attack. He steadied himself and waited for his turn, third on the list. The first wing rocketed ahead, their heat coronas flaring as the moved. Rudy tapped his foot nervously, listening to the coordination between Lieutenant Commander Redding and the leader of Wolf Wing.

"I'm firing in five seconds," Redding's voice echoed in Rudy's helmet. "Fire now!"

The first barrage of heavy rockets departed eight bombers, each craft pulling up and jamming the throttle forward to fall back. This meant Bull Wing was up and they started their run, just as the turrets from the Behemoth opened fire. The resulting blasts rocked the enemy ship, causing their shields to flare so brightly, Rudy had to look away.

They returned fire, unleashing their own version of hell on the Behemoth. Redding moved the craft but it wasn't exactly fast and though she did get them to hit a different section of shielding than the last time, the resulting blast seemed nasty to Rudy. Even if the defenses held, that one had to give everyone on board a good shake.

I hope we're treating these pricks to a similar dance.

Bull wing moved in and the time it took them gave the Behemoth a chance to recharge. Redding's voice came over the line again. "Ten seconds to firing. Count down five and shoot."

"Roger that," Bull Wing replied. "We are ready on your mark. Closing in on optimal range."

"Fire," Redding maintained perfect composure, her tone remaining all business. Rudy didn't know if he could be so calm considering what she was doing. The act of coordinating such a mission made his heart race. If she had any adrenaline rushing through her blood, she didn't let on. *Just one more reason she's got that job, I guess*.

"Opening fire," Bull Wing replied and again, Rudy saw the massive flare up as rockets from all eight craft launched at the enemy. His turn was next and as he watched the enemy get hammered again, he saw them move ever so slightly to the Starboard, away from the attack.

I think we just jarred them! Those pricks are going down!

"Bear wing," Redding said. "Begin your attack run in five seconds."

"Yes, ma'am." Rudy sent the signal to the rest of his wing and counted it down for them. At one, he pressed his throttle forward, peripherally aware of the other ships keeping pace with him. They spread out in a vanguard formation, which allowed them to blanket a larger area with their rockets. As they drew closer, they heard Revente's voice over the line.

"There they come, Cougar and Lion! Get in there and protect those bombers!"

Crap, that means the fighters are here. Just our luck that we get to be the first ones worrying about taking a blast in the face from a bunch of bees.

"Ten seconds on recharge," Redding said. "Get ready to fire."

A fighter flew by Rudy so fast he couldn't tell if it was one of theirs or the enemy's. He didn't risk a look, not even at his scanner. He remained intent on the target, prepared to unleash what he hoped would be the final run on this bastard to take down their shields. The fourth wing's attack definitely had enough force to pop their hull if their defenses dropped.

Coupled with another turret round from the Behemoth and we'd be in serious business.

"Fire," Redding said. "Now."

Rudy gave the order and his wing opened up. He felt the ship jolt upward as his rockets dislodged from the bottom of his ship and jetted forward. "Pull up, everyone and let's get back to the line!"

"Bear One, this is Bear Four, I've got a problem." The message came through as private. Lieutenant Harlon Mitchell had been with Rudy's wing since the beginning. He was a young pilot but damn good at his job. Definitely one of the braver bombers for sure.

"What's the deal, Bear Four?"

"My linkage is jammed. They didn't release the rockets."

"What?" A sense of panic gripped Rudy's chest. "Okay...did they arm?"

"I'm afraid so, sir."

Rudy cursed. "Use your manual over ride! Jettison all ordinance."

"I can't sir, I already tried."

"Bail out, Bear Four. That ship's going to blow."

"I'm arming the rest of my ordinance, sir," Harlon replied. "And ensuring I aim right at the enemy ship."

Rudy hesitated to reply but had to admit the idea was sound. Not only would the bombs do damage but the reactor might mess them up too. If Harlon survived, it would be a miracle though. Bailing out with such a shockwave...his escape pod wasn't exactly equipped with anything more than basic maneuvering thrusters.

Surely not enough to get him a safe distance away from the destruction.

"You bail out and I'll get you out of there," Rudy said. "Just send me your beacon the second you pop the canopy, okay?"

"Sir…" Harlon cleared his throat. "You and I both know that's not practical."

The young man was right. His bomber wasn't fast or maneuverable enough to get the pod out of there in time. They'd likely both die as a result. He checked his com and patched into Lion's wing leader, keeping the channel private for the moment. The fact that it took all of five seconds to connect annoyed him.

"What's up, Bear One?"

"Listen, I need one of you to help Bear Four. His rocket linkage jammed up and he's basically flying a live bomb. He's going to bail out but I can't get him out of there in time. One of you has to do it."

"We can do it," Lion One replied. "I'll lock onto his coordinates and take care of it myself. I trust we're racing a shockwave? Whoa!"

"Lion One, do you copy?" Rudy felt frantic as he and the rest of his wing moved away from the enemy vessel. Blasts danced all around his hull, and he did his best to evade them. Something exploded to his left and he swore it was Bear Four for a moment but then he realized someone just saved his life.

"Yeah, I'm still here, Bear One," Lion One replied. "Sorry, had to kill something. I'll get your guy, don't worry about it. We'll talk later."

Rudy cursed as the man cut the connection and he filled in Revente on what happened.

"Damn...Harlon's going to be okay," Revente said. "Trust Lion One."

"Doing my best...but the next bomber wing's about to head in."

"I know. Just focus on staying alive and getting into position for your next run."

Rudy saw one of the other wings go up, their ship blown to pieces. *No way someone bailed from that ship*. He cursed again, leading his people to the back of the line. The other bombers prepared themselves with five fighters flying around them like gnats. They screened enemy vessels, engaging in wild dog fights not even a hundred kilometers away.

This is insane! They're too close for us to just sit here!

"Sir?" Bear Three spoke up, Flight Lieutenant Luke Broussard. "I'm fairly certain I can get out there and bring Four back. But also...shouldn't we be moving? Evasively at the very least?"

"Stand fast," Rudy said. "We have to trust in our comrades. They've got our backs and won't let us down. Just...have some faith. For Four too."

One of the enemy fighters buzzed so close to Rudy's ship, he swore it nicked him. If they'd been in atmosphere, the sound of its passage would've been deafening. His heart pounded as he waited his wing's turn for another attack. Moving around would only cause more targets, a distraction. Staying put gave their fighters a chance to fight without avoiding a bunch of slow moving obstacles.

A series of explosions all around them lit up Rudy's cockpit, making him wince even with the tinted guard of his helmet. He checked his scanner and watched Bear Four's blip. Harlon spoke to them all, "I'm bailing out now!" His ship was barely a few hundred kilometers from its target when he let them know.

You maniac! Rudy thought. *There's no way you'll get out of the way of that explosion!*

But it made sense. He avoided their countermeasures to get in close, to ensure his ship hit them. Harlon practically sacrificed himself. Bailing out was a token effort, placating desperate hope and luck than any real chance. Rudy scowled, hardening his heart to the reality of the situation. What he just saw, what he was about to witness...valorous as the young man proved to be, hurt the wing commander's heart.

The bomber closed in on its target, dropping below a thousand kilometers. Even if the enemy took the ship out, the explosion would still cause catastrophic damage. Blasts from their turrets turned from the Behemoth to try and save themselves. They even started moving backward in a vain attempt to avoid it.

When the craft smacked into the side, the explosion involved a tremendous blue-purple orb that filled Rudy's entire view ahead of him. When it winked out, he realized any fighters in the vicinity, including Bear Four, would be obliterated. His own scans were knocked offline as a result and as things began to clear, he heard a single static filled message over his radio from Revente.

"Stand down! Wait further orders!"

Damn it! We don't have time to stand down. We need search and rescue! Still, without scanners, they wouldn't find much out there. He had to practice the patience he was so strict about with his pilots. At least for the next few moments, he was forced to take several deep breaths and find some Zen. *We'll come for you soon, Harlon. I promise*.

***

Gray checked the reports after another series of turret blasts struck their shields. They rattled from the blow but didn't seem particularly phased by the attacks. Messages from various parts of the ship corroborated his feeling. A few shorts from hasty repairs earlier but otherwise, all systems showed green.

Incredible luck.

Olly stood, staring at the screen then looking quickly down at his terminal. The suddenness of it would've been comical if the situation weren't so dire. Gray opened his mouth to ask what happened but Redding beat him to it. She was closer and his motion made her jump she was so intent on coordinating the attack.

"What the hell, Darnel? What's wrong with you?"

"Ma'am, one of the bombers is on a collision course with the enemy ship," Olly replied. "It's moving fast!"

"Did it get hit?" Gray asked.

"No, sir. I don't detect that...but every ordinance on board is hot and the reactor is set to overload!"

Gray tapped his communicator. "Revente, come in."

"Yes, sir?" The voice sounded distant in the speaker.

"Are you seeing this bomber careening toward the enemy?"

"That would be Bear Four, sir. Apparently, the linkage holding his bombs froze and his weapons were already armed. His manual override didn't work."

"Meaning it would've blown anyway."

"Yes, sir. Bear Four decided to ram his ship down their throat." Revente sighed. "I authorized the maneuver. He'll be bailing out shortly but..."

"But what?"

"We're not optimistic of his chances to escape."

Gray rubbed his forehead, staring down at the floor. The pilot knew what it meant to be caught in an explosion like what he was about to initiate. Once he hit those shields with all those bombs armed, it would annihilate any unshielded object within ten thousand kilometers...possibly more.

"Understood." Gray turned to Redding. "Let's make that sacrifice mean something. When that thing is close, you hit them hard. Agatha, tell our new friends to get ready to hammer this ship with everything they've got. If this doesn't give us the chance to take them down, nothing will."

"Aye, sir...but..." Agatha hesitated. "It's just, they're pretty busy with the other ship. It's been dishing out some pretty brutal hits."

"I get it but we'll need them to put in whatever they can spare. Revente, when we're done have all available fighters and bombers hit the enemy ship. Together, we should be able to take it down. You got it?"

"Aye, sir. Relaying orders now."

Here we go. This should be it, Gray thought. *Time to finish it off for good.*

Chapter 10

The Behemoth fired their turrets at the same time as all other crafts in the area opened up as well. When Bear Four crashed into the shield, the damage sent a shockwave through the entire enemy vessel, killing generators along the way and lowering the shields. Pulse cannons struck the hull, slipping past anything but the armor.

A few moments passed and the damage done was catastrophic. Bits of the enemy ship flew off as pressure from within separated the broken parts. Bombs hit it from all sides and the fighters strafed it and flew off, avoiding the fighters desperate to stop the constant attack. As the action continued to mount, Raeka watched in awe at the sheer destructive power he faced.

"Open fire on that ship," he ordered softly. "Give it whatever we've got left."

"Yes, sir."

"Send to Darm as well. We need to help as much as we can."

They were engaged with the other vessel but could spare a few ships to throw in some blows. Their own conventional weapons were far less effective against the massive vessel but tiny dots of fire appeared where their mass drivers struck. He considered unleashing a laser blast but it seemed too risky, especially with another enemy *right* there.

A large crack formed in the middle of their target, a black line quickly filled in with orange-red fire. Light erupted from the engines. Earth fighters and bombers flew away, putting some distance between them and what was sure to be quite the wake. Raeka began wondering if they were too close and ordered the few ships who were able to engage to fall back.

A moment passed when he believed they may not have done enough damage. The enemy even fired a few more wild shots from their turrets but they missed any targets. Finally, the hull began to shimmer and a moment later, the brightest light Raeka had ever seen beside a sun filled their monitor.

Light suppression kicked in, preserving their vision but he was still dazzled for several moments. When he blinked away the stars in his vision, he turned to the view port and felt a wave of relief. The enemy vessel was gone. Nothing but massive chunks of debris drifted about where they'd been a moment before.

The other enemy suddenly broke off their attack, reversing thrusters and heading off from the fleet.

"They're retreating!" Gahlir shouted. "They've turned tail to run!"

"I think not," Tarkin said. "They may be pulling away from us, but they're not done with their attack. Check their course. Unless I'm very much mistaken, I believe they're on their way toward the Founder home world."

Gahlir checked his terminal and cursed under his breath. "You're right...but surely they don't think they can do any damage there. Not if we give chase."

"We won't be," Raeka said. "I've got an idea. Put the Behemoth on the line."

"You're live, sir."

"Captain Atwell, this Raeka. I believe that target is yours. They may be heading for one of our planets. If you'd like to give chase, we can perform search and rescue out here. I think we've all got some people drifting we'd like to find."

"Support our shuttles," Atwell said. "They'll help."

"Acknowledged. Good hunting, Captain."

"Appreciate it. Behemoth out."

Raeka gave the order to his people and got Darm on the line. He hoped the man wouldn't need too much convincing to stay put and perform some support. Knowing the Founder commander, it would be some kind of miracle if the conversation went simply. As they looked at each other on the screen, Raeka drew a deep breath and prepared to sell his case.

"We intercepted your transmission," Darm said. "I concur with the Behemoth commander's assessment. We must tend to our ships rather than attempt to chase that thing down."

Raeka tried hard to hide his surprise. "Very well. We'll coordinate with your people to perform search and rescue."

"Indeed. Considering the speed of our adversary, I do not believe we could keep up anyway. Speak to you soon, Raeka."

That's Captain *Raeka*. The thought crossed his mind but a petty squabble about titles seemed pointless. He merely acknowledged and killed the transmission. His own people already worked with the other captains to get their shuttles moving to help the Earth ships find any escape pods which might need help.

Their part of the battle ended, even as the next part began. Raeka felt confident the Behemoth could handle the last one on her own Their captain seemed particularly shrewd. Now to let them do their work. They clearly knew war and their equipment alone spoke of their ability to bring devastation down on their opponents.

I'm quite glad they proved to be on our side. That's a fight I had no interest in losing.

***

"Looks like Bear Four's sacrifice paid off," Olly spoke the words solemnly. "The remaining enemy is moving off. Their fighters are disengaging and returning to join the ship."

"Revente's people are requesting permission to pursue the fighters," Agatha said. "What should I tell them, sir?"

"Disengage," Gray said. "Those are small victories, even if we manage to get a few of them, our people would just be in the way. Get them back aboard as we pursue. Redding, don't let them get away. We *cannot* afford for them to leave this system alive. Are we still jamming their coms?"

Olly nodded. "Yes, sir. A variation on Protocol Seven and a little we learned from the fight at the research facility. They can't get through, especially if they have to diver their attention to fighting us off."

"Good. Pressure them. Pursuit isn't exactly the best position to be in. Keep scans hot and if anything comes up, anything gets in our way, we need to know right away. I'm not in the mood to get surprised by mines or some other booby trap they come up with."

"We're on it."

The Behemoth raced after them, leaving the two fleets behind. Most of the fighters reported in that they made it aboard before full throttle. The others would have to wait with their new allies. Providing they remained hospitable, there was nothing to worry about. Of course, considering the situation, Gray didn't trust them entirely.

Not much choice yet. We'll come back soon enough. Right now, I've got an enemy to eliminate.

***

Marshall insisted Adam leave the arrest up to his people. The commander wanted to be there but the Lieutenant Colonel knew when not to think a situation was simple. He worried their two suspects might not come quietly so he didn't need one of the highest ranking officers aboard to be in harm's way.

Normally, Marshall would call on a couple of regular security personnel to get the job done but he felt this task might require someone a bit tougher. He called upon Captain William Hoffner, who typically only performed away missions. If anyone could bring in the two suspects regardless of their level of resistance, it would be him.

He had Tim moved back to the brig and placed under guard and took up occupancy in the brig's office. While he waited, he checked the location of the two people they were after. Conway was in her quarters and Roper seemed to be on duty in one of the tech labs. At least they weren't off causing mischief.

Marshall had dealt with some pretty rough situations in his career, but traitors never ceased to be the worst. Most of his job involved facing the worst parts of the military, from crimes to ops deep inside enemy lines. If ever something came up that he considered worse, he figured he'd have to retire.

Captain Hoffner showed up and stood at attention as he entered the room, holding his head high. "Reporting as ordered, sir."

"At ease, Captain. I've got an assignment for you, something simple I hope."

"I doubt you think that if you've got me here," Hoffner said. "What's up?"

"We have some saboteurs aboard. One of them identified the other two. We need to arrest them."

"You must think these folks are pretty bad if you're not using MPs." Hoffner scratched his chin. "You anticipate violence?"

"I can't say for sure but I'd like to err on the side of caution."

"Okay, I'll take a couple guys...but we might want to get them at the same time. If they have some friends working in their department, it might spread *really* fast."

"Do whatever you have to. Just make it as quiet as possible."

"Understood, sir. I'll take care of it right now." Hoffner turned to go. "Um...I probably don't really want to know but what's going on?"

"They're the ones who messed up the jump module."

Hoffner stiffened.

Marshall held his hand up. "Just take it easy on them. They're going to have a bad enough day without your guys working them over."

"That's not what I was thinking about...but it's not a bad idea."

"Just bring them in, unharmed if possible. I don't want to hear about some hold out weapon if they don't shoot either."

"Fair enough." Hoffner opened the door. His demeanor suggested Marshall picked the right man. He'd definitely take the proper precautions and ensure they got them both under control quickly. As if to mirror Marshall's thoughts, his parting words solidified his confidence. "We'll be back with them shortly, sir."

***

Rudy received the order to land ASAP but struggled with the order. Search and rescue teams already launched and began their mission. Part of him wanted to join them. He felt responsible for Harlon and didn't want to leave the man behind. They might not find him for hours and if he was injured, it would be far too late.

Of course, Rudy wouldn't be able to do much with him either. He could at least tell the medic ship where to rendezvous. And his ship would at least be capable of attaching to the life pod. The decision was whether or not he wanted to linger and miss the opportunity to land in order to find his missing pilot.

Considering what else is going on, I doubt they'll really notice. I just have to be smart about it. Damn it, Rudy. This is a little crazy.

The Behemoth seemed like it came out on top from the last engagement. They beat the tar out of that first ship, mostly because they went one on one with it. This next one shouldn't prove to be that much harder but there were no advantages this time. No pilot to sacrifice himself.

"Bear One, do you copy? This is hangar control. We're waiting on you, Rudy."

"I'm too far out," Rudy replied. "You're already accelerating. Just remember to come back for me."

"Understood, Bear One. Hangar Control out."

Rudy watched the Behemoth pick up speed, moving rapidly after their fleeing enemy. He didn't waste time considering their departure and instead focused on finding Bear Four. His scanner swept the area, looking for an Earth beacon to lock on to. Sadly, there were several from other wings, bombers and fighters alike.

We didn't exactly get creamed but we lost enough ships! Wow...

He counted fifteen in all but compared to the foreign debris, they definitely came out on top. Experience fighting these guys helped every department. Engineering kept the shields going because they knew what to expect with the energy surges after being attacked. Weapons crews figured out how to cycle the generators to reduce recharge time and the pilots understood the tactics of their chaotic foes.

Rudy began marking the location of their people, broadcasting them on the emergency frequency monitored by search and rescue. They'd have a much easier time finding their folks that way. The two fleets they helped, the new culture that attacked them at first, also seemed to be milling about the area, looking for their own people no doubt.

Someone pinged him from one of the medical shuttles, letting him know they were already collecting life pods. Their ships were equipped with a method to get people aboard making immediate medical attention possible. Rudy continued his search for Bear Four, trying to hone his scanners to only their signature.

It didn't come up. Harlon's chances of surviving that attack were infinitesimal. Miracles happened once in a while but in this case, Rudy had a hard time believing in them, even if they were possible. He clutched his flight stick and moved off toward the mainstay debris of the enemy cruiser where Harlon's pod might've been.

Maybe I can find the debris of it...and at least bring his body back. If he wasn't vaporized. God, what a way to go. He was a real hero. He could've bailed out sooner but he wanted the sacrifice of his ship to be useful. Crazy bastard. Talk about putting the mission before himself. This pretty much embodies that.

Rudy's shields flared up as he approached the chunks of ship, debris burning up before touching his hull. He checked his scanners, still finding nothing. The whole venture made him sick to his stomach. Heading out there should've made him feel better that he was trying *something* rather than sitting on the hangar deck of the Behemoth.

Instead, he just realized how futile the gesture was. He wasn't helping Harlon or anyone else. Maybe a little time away from others would help him come to terms with the loss. But what a stupid situation! Locked linkage? Why? How? Such a malfunction was certainly possible but not entirely probable.

I wish we could get the ship back to find out how it happened. I don't want repeat.

Rudy continued to drift among the debris, ever hopeful his scanners might pick something up. He figured he had some time to kill before the Behemoth came back to get him and the others. He'd spend it wisely, looking for his friend and conjuring up any stories he might be able to tell about him to his comrades.

You'll never be forgotten, Harlon. I promise.

***

Gray gripped the arms of his chair tightly, staring intently at the screen. They were closing on the enemy, coming up on them fast. The other might be able to jump out at any moment so they needed to hit them hard. Knocking out their ability to escape meant keeping their country ignorant of what happened in that system.

Everyone on the bridge kept their heads down, focusing on their work. Olly fed reports back to Gray, different factors of their surroundings and the course the enemy was taking. He also continued to show that their jamming worked. *That's a relief.* If they were able to communicate back to their home base, any attack would be pointless other than removing one more threat from the galaxy.

Even if they can replace these quickly, taking them out is just one more blow to their armada. Each ship we destroy is another one they can't attack us with.

The screen showed the Behemoth veer to port, putting the enemy to their starboard. Gray looked at Redding but before he could ask, she shook her head.

"Acquiring a firing solution on critical systems," Redding said. "Olly, lock in their engine room to the targeting computer."

"Yes, ma'am." Olly went to work and the two coordinated their assault.

Cannons fired, hammering the enemy vessel half way back toward the stern. Their shields held but Redding didn't unleash every weapon at once. She hit them gradually, firing one volley at a time to maximize their firepower through the recharge cycle. Every blast hit the same location with exquisite accuracy.

Okay, she probably deserves a commendation for all she's done in this fight. That was some fantastic shooting.

Gray considered the ordinance their bombers carried and wondered how they could best put them to use. They didn't traditionally rely on shipboard missile firing but the smaller fighters couldn't keep up with what they were doing. Frankly, the bombs might not be able to either. They'd likely fall short of their target because their thrusters wouldn't provide enough speed.

Unless we get out in front of them and let them run into them.

"Redding, what're the chances you can outrun these guys and get out in front of them?"

"I can probably do it," Redding said. "I thought we wanted to prevent them from jumping. We don't want to become an obstacle, do we?"

"Not us, but a bunch of bombs…"

Redding nodded. "Understood, sir. I'm on it."

Gray patched into the hangar. "Hangar Control, I need you to take some bomb ordinance and prepare a few payloads. I'm thinking five warheads each. Get them ready so we can remote arm them. Let us know the moment you're done."

"Yes, sir. We're on it."

"You intend to make mines," Clea said. "Good idea."

"Thank you. If it works, this may well be how we wrap this up."

"The idea came from what the pilot did, am I correct?"

Gray nodded. "To some extent, yes. His entire payload plus the pulse drive took the shields down from the other one. I'm hoping we see the same results with this plan."

"Your hopes tend to come true." Clea turned to her computer. "I'll calculate the number we'll need to bring them down and coordinate with Hangar Control."

"Thanks. I appreciate it."

Gray turned his attention to an incoming message from Adam. *Conspirators have been identified. We are moving in to arrest them now.*

Gray felt his spine stiffen as he wrote back, *who are they and do you know why they did it?*

Lieutenant Theresa Conway, Ensign Amos Roper and Lieutenant JG Timothy Collins. They wanted to stir up trouble between the alliance and Earth. Collins claimed it was Admiral Jameson's idea.

"God damn it," Gray muttered, shaking his head. He'd heard the admiral's anti-alliance rhetoric before and tried to win allies all the time. It didn't even make sense. They saved humanity but he still didn't trust them. Now, he intentionally sabotaged the Behemoth for his cause? That man was going to prison.

How did they intend to make this look like alliance problems?

Adam took a moment to write back but when he did, the words made Gray even angrier. *They intended to frame Clea.*

A woman who sacrificed much to live among humans during one of the most xenophobic times in Earth's history. These people had a lot of nerve and none of it was positive. Gray scowled and looked forward to having a conversation with the three saboteurs, especially Tim. That young man broke his heart.

You threw away a bright future for another man's political schemes. What a waste.

Gray turned to look at Clea. He'd come to think of her as a friend and confidante. They'd worked together since before the refit of the Behemoth. They taught each other much about their respective cultures. She was utterly devastated by her sister's betrayal. No one who knew her would believe her capable of sabotage.

Jameson needed to spend time with the alliance representatives to see how similar they were. His selfish, misguided notions made humanity look like fools. Ignorance such as prejudice might always exist but in this case, it was detrimental to the entire species and the planet. Without alliance support, the Earth would be done.

If he doesn't know that, he doesn't deserve to wear his uniform.

"Sir," Clea interrupted his thinking. "I've done the math and Olly just checked it. I'm afraid we're going to need a *lot* of bombs to do what we're hoping to achieve. Mostly because, correct me if I'm wrong, we want to get this done in one pass."

"Yes, that would be best."

Clea nodded. "Very well. I've had them tether together fifty bombs and they're ready to jettison them on Lieutenant Commander Redding's mark. I can remotely arm them so they'll detonate at the right time. Ultimately, our goal is to disable their defenses. However, secondarily I would like to see their engines taken offline or at least their jump capability."

"Very good." Gray let out a breath and whistled. "Fifty. That's quite the payload. Redding, are we going to be able to get away from that shockwave?"

"It might singe our backside a little," Redding replied. "But I don't see why not. I'll hammer them with the pulse cannons as well."

The Behemoth shook from an attack by the enemy. Gray noted on the view screen that they were pulling ahead. *At least we're faster than them. Never raced one of these guys before. Good to know.* "Looks like they're not happy with being overtaken. Think they know what we're up to?"

"It's not an alliance tactic," Clea said. "We tend to have to wear one another down."

"It's all in your hands, Redding."

Another blast shook the ship and a light flashed brightly enough on Olly's console that it grabbed Gray's attention. He waited for the young man to report on it but figured he knew what he'd hear: shield power reduced. The fact they were pushing the engines to outrun the enemy *and* being hit would take its toll.

Olly confirmed his suspicion, adding, " we're only going to have one or two blasts with the cannons before they need to be recharged at this rate of speed. We're taxing the power reserves as it is."

"Are they ready to get those bombs out there?" Gray asked Clea.

"Yes, sir." Clea checked her readings. "If my calculations are correct, we're going to see quite a show when they go off. Far more destructive than a fighter's pulse core to be sure. I'd say this is overkill but I decided to err on the side of too much."

Olly raised his hand, "I'd just like to say if that payload doesn't obliterate them in one go, they will at *least* be temporarily crippled. That's a lot of destructive power."

"If only we could time delay them, then the shields would absorb the first blow and the second would knock them out." Gray hummed. "Any chance?"

Clea shook her head. "No, because anything we jettison will be annihilated. If the bombs aren't armed or don't go off at the same time, they'll be destroyed before they can. Literally vaporized."

"Well, the turrets can do the rest then." Gray checked their relative position. They'd pulled ahead but only *just*. He wanted a little more space if at all possible. "Are we at full power?"

"And then some," Redding said. "Our engines are approaching redline. We might have to settle for the bombs being detonated near them. If we want the ship to run the payload over, it might not happen. I won't be able to maintain this for long."

"So we'll drop it, veer off and detonate." Gray leaned forward. "We're going to need some specific timing to pull this off. They'll race right by the ordinance otherwise."

"I'll arm them before they leave the ship," Clea said. "I calculate we'll have less than two seconds to detonate to catch them. We are moving *very* fast."

"Wait!" Olly tapped his screen for a moment. "I've got an idea. I can set the bombs to react to their shield frequency! Protocol Seven won't take them down but I still was able to analyze the way they randomize. Because they change theirs differently than we do, it won't blow up next to us but only them."

"How long?" Gray asked.

"Already done. The detonators are programmed into our console per Clea's instructions."

"Sounds good." Gray took a deep breath and leaned back. "I'm pretty sure we're up ahead as much as we can be. Redding, can you buy us any more distance?"

An audible alarm began to sound. Another blow from the enemy shook the ship, this time harder. This brought yet a different alert to the bridge. They were running out of time and needed to take action soon. The next few moments would decide the outcome of the fight for good or ill.

"The first sound you heard was the engines complaining about redlining," Redding said. "I think I've got us out as far as possible from the enemy, sir."

"The second was our shields weakening," Olly added. "Minor damage to crew quarters on decks seventeen and nineteen. We can't take another shot there until the shields charge up."

"And no maneuvering," Gray said. "Okay, Clea, you're up. Get those bombs out there and see what happens. Redding, fire our one blast of turrets on them as you veer off. Once we're at the safe minimum distance, get the engines back to a safe zone and get our guns back up. If we're lucky, the bombs will do all the work but if not...we'll have quite the fight on our hands."

Chapter 11

Clea surprised herself. Her hands trembled as she prepared herself to handle the bombs. Nerves got to her and she didn't exactly know why. She'd been under pressure before but this time was different. If she made an error, she could very well be responsible for the enemy ship's escape.

The calculations were all sound, she triple checked them. She simply needed to hit the button at the right time. Automation might delay even more than an organic hand. This meant she was responsible and it would be fast. The moment she ordered them to release the bombs, she would count one second and detonate.

A split second is really all we have.

Willing her heart beat to slow down did not help. Sweat formed on her brow, tickling the back of her neck. Any moment, Redding would announce that they were prepared and then…

"Go!" Redding shouted. "We're in position but I don't know how long we can hold this!"

Panic threatened to grip Clea's neck and she breathed through it. Clearing her throat, she tried to speak with confidence into her microphone. "Hangar one, this is the bridge. Deploy mine and report the moment it has cleared the ship."

"Mine deploying!" The voice crackling in her ear bud sounded just as nervous as she felt. "Standby!"

The moment of truth. Clea tapped the button to arm the devices. If the soldiers moving the bombs were nervous before, they might well be terrified now. They would be at ground zero for any sort of mishap. Of course, they wouldn't even know what hit them. It would be over in an instant.

The ship shook again as the enemy hammered them with another shot of their turrets. This time, they struck a different shield section so did not cause the amount of damage they could've. Everyone around her performed their jobs without looking even remotely tense. Did they not realize just how dangerous this would be?

At least they have confidence in you. That's something.

"The bomb is clear!"

Clea realized, in less than half a second, her calculations did *not* take into account the time delay between the bomb's deployment and when they reported it was gone. She hit the button, detonating them without the count. A quiet prayer danced through her mind, something from her childhood she hadn't given a second thought for *many* years.

"Detonating!" Redding veered away but when the explosion didn't go off instantly, Clea feared the remote failed.

Please don't say…

When it hit, Clea clapped her hand over her mouth to suppress a yelp. The shockwave slapped them from behind so suddenly the artificial gravity could not keep up. They listed, tilting to what they perceived to be the right. Gray shouted a command to Redding but Clea couldn't hear what he said.

Someone else shouted as the lights went out. Sparks erupted around them from different panels shorting out. As the ship seemed to right itself, Gray shouted over to Olly, demanding a damage report. The young man told him he needed a moment to catch up. The main view screen was off.

We're still alive…that's saying something.

"Engines are using auxiliary power only!" Olly called out. "Weapons are rebooting. We can maneuver but there's no shooting!"

"Shields?" Gray demanded. "How are our defenses?"

"Sections thirty through forty-five are severely damaged, our rear basically!" Olly paused. "We need to get turned!"

"Redding, do you have control?"

"Sluggish, but I'm maneuvering."

"What's the enemy doing?" Gray asked. "Did we take them out?"

"No…but they're not moving either."

"That's why we listed," Clea found her voice. "We lost propulsion and the compensation kicked in to slow us down. They probably have a similar failsafe. If you hadn't veered off, they probably would've run into us."

"Good to know." Gray turned to Olly again. "If you don't get those weapons up before they do, they're going to really cause some devastation."

"I'm on it, sir! They can only recharge so quickly! I'm diverting power while engineering works on the generators."

Clea turned to Gray. "I can get down there and help them out. Permission to leave the bridge."

"Hurry, Clea. We don't have time for mistakes right now."

"Aye, sir. Talk to you in a moment."

Clea hurried to the elevator and slammed the button, bouncing on her feet as it began to descend. Her sense of urgency overwhelmed her earlier nerves. Adrenaline consumed her. This race against time gave her all the thrill she needed for an entire year. When they finished, she fully intended to take a twelve hour rest period and do nothing at all.

I think we've all earned the time off. Now to make sure we get it.

***

Before the Bomb Detonated

Hoffner grabbed Corporal Bobby Jenks, Corporal Dylan Walsh and Sergeant Clint Marsten to arrest the prisoners. The three men were typically reserved for ground missions so sitting out the shipboard action. When he told them they needed to arrest some people, they actually got pumped up at the idea.

Not exactly the reaction I need but not surprising either. These guys hate sitting out in the middle of action.

"You sure they're criminals?" Jenks asked. "I mean, how do we know?"

"We don't," Marsten replied. "Else we'd just put 'em down, right Captain?"

"They've been accused of a crime," Hoffner replied. "Which means they get arrested and tried. But that doesn't mean you don't go in armed. *If* they did what they've been accused of, then they *might* be capable of shooting at you."

Walsh laughed. "To what end? Like they could escape the ship? And where would they go? We're not exactly near a friendly base."

"You're counting on rationality," Hoffner said. "Just be professional, bring them in and call it good, you got it?"

"Yes, sir!" The three men shouted.

"Okay, Jenks, you're with me. We'll get Conway." Hoffner gestured to the others. "You two get Roper. He's at his post in Tech Lab Six."

"We'll get him," Marsten said. "See you back at the brig, sir."

Hoffner led the way down to the crew quarters, drawing his weapon once the elevator opened. Jenks followed suit, losing some of his swagger as soon as they faced the actual assignment. That's why he was picked for the duty. The man knew when to shut up and get down to business.

They approached Conway's door, taking either side of it. Hoffner knocked, electing to do the talking.

"Lieutenant Conway, this is Captain Hoffner. We need you to open the door and come out slowly with your hands raised. Do you copy?"

No reply.

"Maybe she's not home," Jenks muttered.

Hoffner pulled his mobile computer and checked the logs for her room. It stated she should be present. "This thinks she's here," he replied. "Let's get in there and check."

He used his security override to unlock the door and remotely opened it, pausing a good five seconds before peeking inside. As a lieutenant, she had a private room though it wasn't quite as spacious as some of those shared by ensigns. Her bed was neatly made, the desk in perfect order and the bathroom door was wide open.

Not here. Hoffner scowled, considering the room for a long moment. *We should be able to find her with the directory. But if she's up to no good…*

"Check in with Walsh while I find out where Conway is."

"You got it."

Hoffner tapped into the directory and started a search. With all the network activity, it seemed like it was going to take a moment. He clenched his fist, frustrated but diverted his attention to hear how Walsh and Marsten did. Hopefully, Roper really did show up for duty and was actually there.

And not hanging out with Conway causing trouble.

***

Walsh and Marsten arrived in the tech lab about the same time Hoffner and Jenks hit Conway's room. They entered to strange looks but no one said anything. Walsh looked at Roper's picture on his hand computer but didn't see him in the crowd. The two soldiers exchanged a glance before Marsten took the lead.

"Alright, jack asses! We're not here cause we're bored. Where the hell's Ensign Roper? He's supposed to be on duty right now."

"He didn't show up," one of the techs replied. "We assumed he hit the medical bay after everything that happened."

"Oh, you assumed that did you?" Marsten shook his head. "No one called on him? Where's the supervisor here?"

"Ill, sir." Another tech answered this time. "He called in to say he was confined to a bed after the event."

"God damn it." Marsten stepped away just as their communicators went off.

"It's the captain and Jenks," Walsh said. He established the connection. "What's going on? Did you get her?"

"No," Jenks replied. "How'd you do with Roper?"

"He ain't here." Walsh sighed. "And his coworkers aren't exactly any help. His supervisor's down...we need to do a directory search to find these two yahoos. Especially if neither of them are where we expected."

"The captain's way ahead of you," Jenks said. "Give him a moment."

The ship suddenly listed. Techs hit the ground. Walsh stumbled into Marsten who grabbed the wall and kept them aloft. Everything rattled as the lights went out. The first thought to drift through Walsh's head involved a simple *this is it, this is where we all die*. When it didn't happen immediately, he wondered how long it would take to run out of air.

The techs started panicking, screaming incoherently while the two soldiers made their way into the hallway. Walsh tapped his communicator to see if it was still functional, yelling into it. "Hey! Jenks, can you hear me? Come in, do you copy?"

"Yeah, I've got you," Jenks said, coughing a few times. "What the hell was that?"

Hoffner answered, "something big...something more than enemy fire, that's for sure. What, exactly, I don't know though. We need to hurry and find these two ASAP. God knows they might've even been involved."

"Not exactly what I want to hear," Marsten said. "Let's meet up, guys. I'm pretty sure they're going to be together anyway."

"Sure enough," Hoffner said. "Looks like they're heading for engineering. Let's hook up in corridor C and head in together. Double time it, people. We'll see you soon."

***

Gray got on the com to Revente. "Any fighter or bomber wings ready to go? Are the hangars operational?"

"I've got people still in their ships just in case, but—"

"We need them up right away."

"I was going to say I'm not sure it's a good idea to send them straight out after that attack. I don't know what's damaged and what's not. We're running diagnostics at this very moment."

"If we don't get an advantage in this fight right away, it might not matter." Gray checked his computer. "Shields are weakened on our ship and *may* be down in theirs. I guarantee you they're about to launch fighters now can you get me some air support or what?"

"I'll get them out there, sir," Revente replied. "Don't worry."

"Let me know when they're out there." Gray turned to Redding. "How's helm?"

"Thrusters are all operational," Redding reported. "We're back online and I'm repositioning now."

"Power output from the enemy vessel?" Gray asked.

"Minimal," Olly replied. "But it seems to be increasing. I don't think they'll be jumping anytime soon. Their shields are currently down...as in totally down. But our weapons are still recharging."

"Check on engineering," Gray said. "See if there's anything you can do from here for them. We need those weapons back to finish this off. I only hope fighters are enough to do the trick if we can't."

"Um...this is odd." Olly tapped at his controls. "Agatha, can you try to reach engineering? They're not responding."

"To me either, lieutenant," Agatha replied. "They seem to be blocked."

"Blocked?" Gray turned in his seat. "What exactly do you mean by that?"

"Someone's jamming their coms...from the source."

"As in the jamming is coming *from* engineering?" Gray tilted his head. "That doesn't make any sense unless...Oh God. Olly, get Clea on the line now. I'm reaching out to Adam. I have a bad feeling we just caught up to our saboteurs and in just the way we hoped not to."

***

Clea burst from the elevator and nearly ran into one of the medics trying to board. She slipped away and ran, dodging past people in the hallway lingering about from injury or trying to repair shorts. Ahead, she saw the corridor leading to the engine room and put on a burst of speed, feeling her heart pound heavy in her chest.

"Hold on!" Maury's voice made her slow down and pause. "Just...listen to me, put the weapon down. This is unnecessary! We've got this fight in the bag! No one has to die...least of all the *entire* ship!"

Clea frowned, creeping forward until she could peek inside. She saw someone's back and a weapon aimed at the engineers. Maury stood in front of them, his hands raised as he tried to talk the culprit down. *What exactly is this all about? The saboteurs? It must be! But why? Are they suicidal?*

"Just relax, Maury," the woman with the gun spoke. Clea didn't know her. "This will all be over in a moment."

"The way I see it," another technician spoke up, "there's no reason to stand here. Get shot by you or blown up by the enemy? What kind of choice is that?"

"The one you're making right now," the woman replied. "Now just stay put! We're almost done."

Clea considered a weapon but the armory was quite a ways off. By the time she got back, these maniacs would be done. She needed to come up with something *immediately* if she hoped to prevent whatever new disaster they wanted to leverage against the ship. It might even involve a really stupid risk.

When her com buzzed, she cursed under her breath and faded back from the door, tapping it to kill the volume. Clea held her breath as she waited to see if the lady heard her and a moment later, her worst fear came true. "Did you hear that, Roper?"

"No, I'm a little busy, Conway. Jesus, can you just shut up?"

"I thought I heard a com unit in the hallway."

"There are a lot of people running around," Roper replied. "I'm sure you did. Now shut up!"

"You're both insane!" Maury shouted, clearly trying to distract them. "Do you have any idea what you're doing here?"

Thank you, Maury! Clea thought. She moved a ways back and answered her com unit in a whisper. As she did so, she pressed herself into a door to remove herself from casual view. "This is Clea."

"Clea, it's Gray. We lost contact with the engineering section. Be careful!"

"I nearly walked right into it," Clea replied. "There's a woman holding a gun and someone named Roper. They're holding the engineers hostage and doing something."

"That would be Lieutenant Theresa Conway and Ensign Amos Roper," Gray replied. "They're the saboteurs responsible for the jump module fiasco."

"Understood. I don't have a weapon, sir."

"It's okay," Gray said. "I let Adam know there was a problem down there. He and Marshall were about to arrest these two maniacs. The soldiers are on their way. Hang tight and don't do anything crazy, copy?"

"Copy, sir. An'Tufal out."

Clea peeked back down the hall, trying to see anything going on in there. She heard Maury talking again, this time more frantically. "Get your hands off that, you stupid son of a bitch! You'll kill us all!"

"That's kind of the point," Conway replied. "Now, if you want to die right now, keep talking. I've had enough of your shit anyway."

"What the hell happened to you? How could you do this?"

"The alliance will destroy our culture, our species," Conway said. "We need the people of Earth to rise up and say *no* to working with these things. They're aliens and we just welcomed them into our lives."

"They saved our lives, you psycho!" Another technician yelled it.

"Did they?" Conway laughed. "Did you ever stop to think that they might be responsible for those creatures showing up on our doorstep? They took an interest in us and then, shortly after the enemy arrived and tried to kill us all. I don't call that a coincidence."

"Took an interest?" Maury scoffed. "Where are you getting these lies from? I never heard anything like that! They came when they found out a technologically advanced culture was going to rip us a new one! I'd call them altruistic!"

"Then why did they only leave *one* person behind? Why not give us some more support to help refit the Behemoth? No, they didn't. They rushed back off to do God knows what elsewhere. All around, it sounds suspicious to me. Only a blind idiot would think there's not some conspiracy."

Conspiracy? Clea shook her head. *What is she even talking about? She clearly didn't read anything we provided. This is how we operated with every culture we brought into the alliance. Of course, I guess if you're trying to build a case against us, it makes sense to do so this way. Still, it holds no rationality, no weight. What a ridiculous waste of time!*

"An'Tufal?" Hoffner's harsh whisper made her jump but she hurried down the hall to meet him and the other four. "What's going on? Do you have any intel?"

Clea nodded. "There are two people in there at least. One is armed and holding the technicians hostage. The other is performing some kind of sabotage...we need to hurry!"

Hoffner scowled and gestured down the hall. "Alright, guys get down there but try to do it quietly. I don't want her shooting at us until we're ready for her to."

"Rules of engagement?" Jenks asked.

"If Conway shoots, incapacitate her. If that means she dies, then so be it. I'll take the heat for it." Hoffner looked at Clea. "You'll want to hang back if you don't have a gun."

"I don't...but I'll stay nearby to help when it's over."

"Good." Hoffner followed the other soldiers and Clea watched from her vantage, leaning against the wall to witness the action. Hopefully they'd take care of the two quickly. Such things usually only took a few moments. Especially when the people tended to be trigger happy. After seeing those men in action on the research facility, Clea doubted Conway would be walking out of there.

***

Hoffner let the others take point, watching as they took position on either side of the door. He approached, using the corner as cover. A little negotiation might help and then he could fulfill his directive of bringing them back alive. If she didn't want to talk, well...Jenks was a damn fine shot. He'd take her down.

"Conway," Hoffner yelled. "What the hell are you doing?"

"Captain?" Conway sounded surprised. "What are you here for?"

"You and Roper," Hoffner replied. "Collins gave you up. Surrender. I don't want to have to shoot you."

"Don't be ridiculous, we're almost done!"

"I don't care what you're doing, but I do care about your life. If you don't put your weapon on the deck and come out with your hands up in a moment, we're going to end you. I'm pretty sure you know I'm not lying."

"Maybe you forget the fact I have hostages. I guess I can prove to you how serious we are."

"No wait!" Maury shouted just as a gun went off. The chief engineer cried out and a moment of people shouting ended with a harsh command from Conway.

"Anyone else wants to get shot, just keep talking! Come here, you!"

"She's using one of them as a shield," Jenks said. "Shot Higgins in the stomach."

Hoffner clenched his fist, fighting back rage. "You just ended your life, Lieutenant! I hope all this was worth it to you!"

"To save the human race, of course it is! Now back off or this guy's dead!"

"If I back off, then everyone on board dies." Hoffner made eye contact with Jenks then Marsten. They nodded to Walsh. The silent message told them what to do: breach in five seconds. "Even if I have to take that poor bastard to get to you, I have no choice. You realize that, right? I have no choice. You've pushed my hand to this."

"Do what you have to do. I'll take at least one of you with me!"

"Roper! You want to die too? You that dedicated to the cause?" Hoffner shook his head. "Something tells me you're not as brainwashed as this psycho!"

"Shut up!" Roper shouted. "Just shut up!"

Before he finished his rant, Jenks and Walsh rushed the door, weapons raised. They both fired at the same time. Conway shot back. Hoffner followed with Marsten close beside him. They breached the room to find Higgins lying on the floor with two men applying pressure. Conway fled deeper into the engineering section and the shield she held was lying on the floor, unconscious.

Roper worked the controls of one of the modules, not even slowing down when they got in there. Hoffner aimed his weapon at the man. "Stand down, Roper! That's an order!"

"He's not going to," Marsten said.

Hoffner sighed, shooting him just above the knee. Roper screamed and collapsed to the ground, gripping his wound and panting. "No! You can't! I have to finish! You don't understand, if this fails, they'll kill my family! I have no choice!"

"Take him into custody," Hoffner pointed. "An'Tufal, get your ass in here and look at what he was doing. Walsh, get a medical team down here stat. Jenks, you're with me. Let's hunt this Conway bitch down and finish the mission."

"How far could she possibly have gotten?"

One of the technicians looked up from Higgins. "There are access ladders to other decks down there. Maintenance tunnels mostly."

"Fantastic!" Jenks rolled his eyes. "I say we go on ship wide alert. Get every security guy on board looking for her."

"I'm ahead of you," Hoffner replied, putting out the call. "She won't get far now."

Clea burst into the room, pausing when she noticed the blood. Hoffner recognized an expression of shock take her face and he hurried over, grabbing her by the shoulders. "Hey! You don't have time for that. Snap out of it and get to work. Undo whatever that prick was doing! You've got him for another moment if you can make him talk."

Hoffner had to give her a quick shake to bring her back to reality. "I'm not kidding, An'Tufal! Get your head back in the game!"

"Sorry, sir." Clea moved over to the console and looked it over. "This is the shield control array. He was messing with our frequencies...oh no..."

"What?" Marsten asked as he finished cuffing Roper. "You want me to make him talk?"

"No, I see what he was doing. He was going to make it so any blow to our shields from a pulse weapon would cause a chain reaction...essentially, one hit would detonate our core. Instead of reflecting the damage, it would be redirected and cause feedback. The overload would essentially destroy the ship."

"Great job, asshole." Marsten nudged Roper with his foot. "Glad you made that decision for all of us."

"Get him to the brig," Hoffner said. "Can you fix it, Clea?"

Clea nodded. "I just need to know precisely what he did. I need everyone else working on getting the generators back so we have weapons. If we're shot in the next few minutes, we'll all be dead. It would be good if we fired first."

"We're after Conway," Hoffner added. "Good luck, Clea. Talk to you soon."

"I do hope so, Captain." Clea frowned at the controls. "For all our sakes."

Chapter 12

Adam arrived on the bridge just as he received the report of what went down in the engineering area. He rubbed his eyes as he took his seat, turning to Gray to update him. So many events were transpiring at once, he felt like an ass having to bring this issue up but a runaway traitor with a gun was definitely a factor to consider in a battle.

He gave him the update, finishing with the bad news about Maury being shot. Gray wore a neutral expression until he heard about the chief engineer's injury. Even then, he just scowled but Adam had known him long enough to recognize the rage boiling just beneath the surface. The captain was a fairly good tempered man but when his ire was stirred, he tended to become uncompromising.

When he told him what the two saboteurs were doing, Adam thought he might blow a gasket.

"Will Maury be okay?" Gray kept his voice low.

"The medics have him but it's too soon to say. They'll report to me when they have something."

"And Conway?"

"Hoffner and his people are in pursuit. He's also initiated a security alert. She's being hunted by every able bodied man on the ship."

Gray nodded. "Okay. Lock down the bridge just in case."

Adam tapped the controls set into his chair and a pair of audible clicks resounded from each door. He took a deep breath and turned his attention to the action reports from the battle to see where they were at. Much had happened since he started his investigation and now, he realized how dire the current situation had become.

"Chances of getting weapons back up?" Adam asked.

Gray shrugged. "Good in that regard but I guess it depends on Clea now. If she's not successful, and we're slow to fire...."

"Hoffner reported she was on it," Adam replied. "So there is that."

"I have faith in her. But just now, I'm not feeling particularly optimistic."

Adam remained silent, turning his attention to reports from all over the ship. The busy work helped him stay focused and bolstered his patience. Everyone was busy doing their jobs. No need to get in the way. Whether they succeeded or not had nothing to do with leadership. Only the skill and talent of the men and women working would get them through now.

Adam knew when to stay out of the way.

***

Clea's fingers flew over the controls of the console, moving with a precision that shocked her. Roper's sabotage was obvious on the surface but undoing it required finesse. Had he been allowed to finish, the results may have been irreversible. She wondered where he got the expertise to create such a problem, where he got the training.

Luckily, he'd been shot. His blood remained plastered over the wall beneath the console. The coppery scent turned her stomach, trying to distract her. Even as she worked, she recognized she was standing in a small pool of blood, enough droplets to make the floor feel sticky through her boots.

Focus. You have to get this problem solved.

Somehow, Roper gained access to Protocol Seven and utilized it to reverse the shields, to turn them into a bomb rather than the defenses they were supposed to be. He rewrote the computer code governing them, altering it destructively without a backup to the original. Fortunately, they kept all the computer code in a repository to avoid mistakes.

However, she still needed to find *all* the modules he altered. That's what took time and she needed to check every reference. Even one mistake might mean the destruction of the Behemoth. She read swiftly, using her own application to scan the others. Doubling up made it possible but it became apparent Roper arrived prepared.

He must've rewritten the code elsewhere and just been installing it. If he'd been a little more efficient, he would've finished in no time. Thankfully, he must've been unfamiliar with the interface. Incredible luck for us.

Clea ran simulations all the way through to ensure she fixed each module. One of the nearby technicians checked the code, calling out when he found errors. The two of them were able to pass through several of the modules in only a few minutes. They needed to cover a dozen more then run a final test to ensure the shields were ready for combat.

Meanwhile, the lights flashed overhead, a side effect of the security alert as they tried to find Lieutenant Conway. Clea figured no one would be particularly kind to her when she was caught. She didn't blame them. Maury Higgins was one of the nicest men on board. The fact she so callously shot him for no reason made her earn any punishment she suffered.

Eleven to go. Come on, Clea. Hurry! Hurry!

***

Hoffner, Jenks and Marsten arrived at the maintenance corridors where Conway could've gone up or down. They paused there, checking their computers to see if they got a hit on her location. Somehow, she'd managed to avoid running past a camera or check point. She must've been hiding out somewhere in the maintenance tunnels.

"She might be prepping an ambush," Marsten said. "We've got her contained, don't you think?"

Hoffner shook his head. "No, as long as she's free to roam around here, she's a threat. We can't consider her neutralized until she's in custody."

"So what're we going to do?" Jenks asked. "Split up?"

"I think so," Hoffner replied. "We have to cover ground. Marsten and I will go up. Jenks, go find some backup and head down."

"No disrespect, sir," Jenks said, "but I don't think we've got time to get back up, do we?"

"She can't cause the same trouble her buddy was trying to do," Hoffner said. "The worst thing she's got in her now is hurting someone."

"That's pretty bad," Marsten pointed out.

"Jenks, I'm not letting you go down there alone. Now, get some damn back up and we'll do this right."

"Yes, sir." Jenks hurried off.

Marsten started up the ladder without prompting, letting his gun lead the way. Hoffner tensed up. Taking a ladder was one of many tactical nightmares. When the sergeant poked his head through the hole, there was always the chance that their target could just take a shot, killing the poor bastard before he had a chance to do anything about it.

When he didn't hear a gun go off, Hoffner relaxed and followed him up. Once they reached the next level, a tight passage allowing access to various systems throughout the ship, they started moving down as quickly as the close quarters allowed. Hoffner had to duck but Marsten was just short enough that he could make it without risking a knock on the head.

They made it to a junction that headed off to the left or right. Marsten crouched, scrutinizing the ground as Hoffner stood overwatch. He didn't detect any movement in either direction. She had to have come through this way but did she go left or right? What was her intention? He checked the schematic really fast and saw that one could get to the elevator shaft to the left or the mess hall to the right.

From the mess hall, she could get to crew quarters or even one of the hangar bays. And that didn't take into account the elevator. *Okay, so did she want to climb around in an active shaft or go somewhere with a chance of escape?*

"She didn't go left. Come on."

"How do you know?" Marsten stood and followed him. "There's a chance…"

"A hunch. I think she wanted options. Climbing the elevator shaft wasn't a logical one."

They picked up the pace, jogging until they reached an access door that led into the hallway. It was open, pried by one of the emergency bars. Someone screamed off in the distance, Hoffner guessed a good hundred meters away. A gun went off and he cursed, breaking into a full run.

They arrived on a scene where three people hovered around a fourth who was on the ground, holding his gut. *What is it with this chick and gut shots?*

Hoffner contacted Jenks on the com. "Jenks, we're in pursuit of the target. Standby."

"Are the medics on the way?" Marsten asked.

"Yes, sir." One of the three replied. "We called them right away and are applying pressure."

"Which way did she go?" Hoffner added. "Do you know?"

"That way," two hands pointed down a hall leading to the hangar. "She's crazy!"

"We get that." Hoffner nudged Marsten. "Let's go. Heading to the hangar can't be good. Jenks, meet us in Hangar Three ASAP."

"Got it, sir." Jenks replied.

Marsten fell into step beside him. "You don't think she's crazy enough to try and steal a fighter, do you?"

Hoffner shrugged. "Probably. Let's go find out."

***

Meagan did not anticipate getting back out in space after what her fighter had been through. As she waited for clearance to launch in a different fighter than her own, she checked the roster of pilots coming with her. Instead of her whole wing, she found herself with only three others and two bombers. It was all they could quickly muster after they last boarded.

She wished that Rudy had come back. It would've made her feel better to be flying with him. All the years they served together made her feel comfortable with him. These other folks were good, but they'd only met when they started their tour aboard the Behemoth. Still, their whole goal was to hit the enemy hard while they were down, to buy some time.

Shields down, weapons down...this is a nightmare situation.

Revente gave them clearance to launch and they gunned it, popping out of the hangar and turning hard to starboard. As they brought the enemy into view, she marveled at the darkness of the hull. None of the usual lights illuminated from the various windows. For all intents and purposes, it looked dead.

"Precision hits," Revente's voice piped into their speakers. "That's what you're after. Go for the midsection where the engineering section is. Keep those shields offline. Bombers, drop them on the thrusters. If they can't maneuver, we've won."

"I'll patch in with you guys," Meagan said. "Fighters, when those bombs are let loose, hall ass away. You do *not* want in on that destruction. You get me?"

"Yes, ma'am!" The response from so many people at the same time hurt her ears. She narrowed her eyes and focused on the target, allowing her computer to show her exactly where to shoot. The first strafing run felt surreal as they hammered the hull of the enemy craft without so much as a shot fired in return.

Bulbs of fire erupted from the surface as they passed by. She didn't even have to use evasive maneuvers as she turned for a second run. They truly were down and out. *This is just a matter of semantics. If we can hit this thing hard enough, it'll be over before we know it. I guess we didn't need more pilots after all.*

The bombers moved in, firing their payloads toward the engines just as the fighters began a second strafing run. By the time the bombs arrived, the fighters would be far enough away to avoid too much damage. Meagan hit the afterburners after she cleared the enemy, allowing herself to relax while racing away from the impact.

"Oh my God!" One of the bombers shouted. "Panther One, I have a problem. Enemy fighters—"

The rest of his message turned to static and she glanced over her shoulder in time to see his ship get vaporized by an enemy ship, flying in erratic circles. *I guess they're in the exact same boat as us...makes sense that they'd follow suit.*

"Group Commander Revente," Meagan called out. "We're going to need some reinforcements. Enemy fighters have engaged. We're down one bomber but their payloads were deployed and..."

The explosion cut her off, jamming her radio with the sudden shockwave that spread out in all directions. The enemy capital ship careened, drifting away from the concussion blast. Static danced across their engines and a bout of flame erupted in a strange oval globe, flaring every so often.

Well that worked.

"Direct hit!" Mick called out. "Their engines are done!"

"They're still dangerous," Revente said. "Engage those fighters. I'm going to try to get you some more people out there but for now, you have to keep those things away from the Behemoth. We're still not in a position to fight them. Repeat, keep those fighters at bay. Copy?"

"Copy," Meagan said. "We'll take care of it as best we can but reinforcements are pretty much essential."

"I'm recalling the bomber. He's not going to do anymore good out there."

If he makes it back, Meagan thought. Chances were slim. She also felt a flare of annoyance. She'd already survived uneven odds once that day. A second time felt especially unfair. *I figured I was done with fighting for an afternoon too. Fate's being a particular bitch today I guess.*

"Come on, Mick. Let's take the lead and keep these jerks off the ship. I hope this isn't a repeat of earlier today."

"If it is, we know we were meant to die out here."

"That doesn't work for me," Meagan replied. "So stow the pessimism and start shooting. I plan on making it home after all this."

***

Olly slapped the arm of his chair and cursed loudly. "We got their engines and they aren't raising their shields but they're maybe a minute away from weapons still! How do they do it?"

"Generators for each system?" Redding asked. "I can get us out of here."

"Get us moving," Gray said. "If we're at extreme range, they won't be able to do much but take potshots and I'm pretty sure we can survive a few of those." He patched down to the engineering section. "Clea, we have to move. How're you doing on getting those shields fixed?"

"Another two minutes at most," Clea replied.

"You have one, see what you can do." Gray turned to Agatha. "Give them a chance to surrender. Send it out on all frequencies. We've never done this before but maybe these guys are feeling a little less than excited about dying horribly."

"Yes, sir."

"They're not even going to respond," Adam said. "And if they can shoot us, you damn well know they're going to do it."

Gray shrugged. "We try everything and besides, returning with some prisoners would definitely do wonders with the brass. It could make this side trip worth quite a lot. Anyway, no time to slow down now, ladies and gentlemen. Keep your focus. This isn't over yet."

***

    Hoffner and Marsten arrived in the hangar and slowed before entering, aiming their guns through the door. They didn't hear anything going on inside. As far as Hoffner knew, they were using this particular hangar to repair the ships damaged in the last fight. It was mostly full of vessels needing attention and the techs were busy in one of the other ones, supporting the fight outside.

    Still, a couple people had to be in there working. But considering the silence, Hoffner felt something was off. Conway was in there somewhere and she probably wanted to get out. How insane would she be? He couldn't wait to find out. "We should wait for Jenks and his guy," Hoffner said. "This is a big area to cover for two people."

    "If she's in a fighter?"

    "Then she's as good as gone anyway," Hoffner replied. "We can't stop her from leaving if she's already inside a ship."

Jenks pinged them to say he was thirty seconds out. Hoffner leaned against the wall, using it for cover. Half a minute could be a lifetime in a combat situation but it felt even longer when nothing seemed to be happening. The tension made him want to tap his foot and he refrained, staring into the hangar intently for any sign of movement or sound.

Then it came. Someone cried out. A scuffle went on. A man shouted for help. Marsten cursed and Hoffner nodded to him. The two men darted inside, moving for toward the sound. They rounded a bomber to find Conway holding a technician from behind. She'd dragged him backward so he was off balance and she placed her gun against the side of his head.

"You guys are persistent," Conway said. "I guess I shouldn't be surprised."

"No, you really shouldn't." Hoffner aimed his gun at her face. "It's over, Conway. Let him go and give it up already. I'm sick of chasing your ass."

"I'm leaving this ship, Sir." Conway shook her head. "And you can't stop me."

Marsten scoffed. "The hell we can't! Put that gun down or we're going to take you out!"

"Neither of you would risk this man just to put me down. If I leave with a fighter, what's it matter? It's not like I'm going to get far. You both know it. But I'd rather die out there than be executed for sabotage and treason."

"You probably won't make it to trial at this rate," Hoffner said. "I'm going to give you one last warning then I'm going to shoot."

"Don't bluff me!" Conway pressed the barrel hard into the man's head. "He dies if you keep pushing me!"

"You got her, Marsten?" Hoffner asked.

"Yes, sir. On your word."

"Believe me," Hoffner said. "He doesn't miss and you know that. You've seen him shoot before. Jenks is on the way and you *know* he's a good shot. I might not be as great but here's the thing, I'm less than fifteen feet away and guarantee I'll hit something. Consider the fact that I don't want you to get away no matter what. That should tell you I'm not bluffing."

"To hell with you, Hoffner!" Conway shoved the man away and began to turn her weapon on them. Marsten fired, Hoffner pulled the trigger and a third gun went off. Conway danced away from both of them, slamming hard into the hull of a nearby fighter. Her head jerked back and she collapsed to the ground, her torso covered in blood.

Jenks rushed over and kicked her gun aside, aiming at her head. "Clear!"

"Thank you, Corporal," Hoffner approached and crouched beside her. She stared up, barely able to move. Her breathing was labored and he knew without even touching her, she had moments to live. "So was it worth this?"

Her mouth opened to reply but nothing came out. Hoffner nodded and stood, turning to the others. "Get someone down here to take her to the morgue. I'll report to Lieutenant Colonel Dupont. We're done here...all of us."

***

Adam turned to Gray. "Report just in from Marshall. They got the traitors. One of them wouldn't go down without a fight but the other is in custody and receiving medical treatment."

Gray nodded. "Very good. One dilemma down, two to go."

"There's quite the dogfight going on out there, sir," Olly said. "We seem to be winning for now...I suspect they have a disadvantage."

"Why do you say that?" Adam asked.

"Whenever their ships are damaged, their fighters don't do as well in combat," Olly replied. "I noticed it when we were at the research facility. Like they receive considerable tactical assistance from their mother ship."

"Fascinating." Gray rubbed his chin. "How close are they to firing?"

"Oh, they're..." Olly stiffened. "Sir...their weapons are online. Preparing to fire."

"Are we out of range yet?" Gray turned to Redding. "Tell me we're out of range!"

"Pretty far," Redding said. "I'd estimate...borderline extreme range with them, sir."

"Ensign White, ship wide warning," Gray said. "Brace for impact. This is probably going to hurt."

***

Clea finished the final module and turned to the technician. "Well?" She asked. "Are we going to explode?"

"One moment, ma'am."

"We don't have a moment," she insisted. "Finish the test! Speed it!"

"I'm working as fast as I can!" He cried. "Wait! I...it's done! It shows green!"

"Are you sure?" Clea moved over beside him and checked the results. The test completed successfully. They'd fixed the shields. *Not a moment too soon!* She rushed back to her console and slapped a button, powering up the shields to cover the ship. *If we were wrong, we won't have long to lament it.* "Clea to bridge, do you copy?"

"We're here," Gray said, "I hope you have some good news?"

A message broadcast throughout the ship from Ensign White. "Brace for impact. Incoming enemy fire!"

"I'm raising the shields as we speak! Estimated time to full defenses, less than ten seconds!"

She heard Gray ask aloud, "how long before they fire?"

"They're firing!" Olly shouted. "Right now! First shots...clean misses!"

"Keep tracking!" Gray yelled. "Redding!"

"I'm moving as fast as I can, sir! This isn't a fighter!"

Clea held her breath, tapping her computer into the bridge scanners. She watched as a blast nearly connected with the Behemoth, skimming the hull. The next one would be a direct hit. It raced against the defenses, half a second would tell whether they took a dangerous blow or allowed the shields to absorb the impact.

A light flared outside. The shields came up, defending them from the blast. Technicians cheered around her and she relaxed her shoulders, slumping against the wall. *We did it! I can't believe we did it.*

"Great work, Clea!" Gray shouted. "Now, get me some weapons so we can finish this son of a bitch off!"

"We're on it, sir." Clea turned to the other technicians. "You heard the captain, guys. Divert all available power to the weapons. Let's win this battle so we can go home!"

***

Raeka watched his screen intently, the magnification at maximum. He witnessed the dramatic explosion of something striking the enemy vessel and both ships slowing to square off. Tiny flares of action erupted moments later then blasts from the nearly defeated enemy. The Behemoth pulled away, evading the attacks...then dramatically deflecting one as their shields came back online.

This is an intense fight.

The others on the bridge seemed just as awe struck by the action, waiting on the edges of their seats to see how it played out. Raeka put his money on the Behemoth. They'd been daring and wily so far. He had no reason to believe they'd be anything but during this all out brawl.

They need weapons. The enemy seems to still have no shields! Maybe we can help.

"Helm, how long would it take to get out there?"

"Over an hour at this distance, sir. I don't even know how they got that far so fast."

Their technology is out of control, Raeka thought. "Even the scouts?"

"We'd be there long after the fight ended."

"Understood." He sat back in his chair and watched, helpless and frustrated for it. Even if the humans didn't win, the Emancipated fleet was safe. The enemy was all but combat ineffective at this point. They could just cruise over there and finish it off. *Which we should start planning on doing just in case*. "Lay in an intercept course. Just in case. Leave search and rescue. I want to be there in case this doesn't go our way."

***

Meagan flipped her fighter and took out one of the enemy vessels. She barely pulled off the maneuver, the ship she was flying didn't quite have the same feel as her own. Mick came up behind her and saved her from an attacker on her six. They raced off together, looking for more trouble.

***

Olly watched the power climb in the weapons, recharging faster than he'd ever seen. They were nearly there. He turned to Redding. "Seventy percent and climbing. I recommend we get into position for optimal firing range."

"Captain?" Redding asked. "Permission to close?"

"Granted," Gray said. "Let's get in there and finish them off."

They lumbered toward the enemy, picking up the pace. Adam spoke into his microphone. "Revente, tell the pilots to disengage and start back toward us. We're about to make the final push."

"This is it," Gray said. "You ready, Redding?"

Redding nodded. "Weapons are online in five...four...three...two...one...Ready to fire on your mark, sir."

"Fire when ready."

Redding took a moment to aim, getting the targeting computer to help. She narrowed her eyes and leaned forward as she stared at one of the screens on her console. As she pulled the trigger, she held her breath and so did Olly who watched her intently. The ship hummed and rattled as every turret fired at the same time.

They watched the screen as pulse blasts lit up space. They struck the unshielded enemy directly on the side, splitting it in the center like an egg. A massive crack opened in the hull and it began to separate, flames filling in the gaps. Redding turned the ship and used the maneuvering thrusters to get them away, giving them some space for when the enemy core blew.

A moment passed before the entire enemy ship went up in blue-purple flames. It flared for a good minute before going out, leaving behind only debris and ashes. Olly let out a whoop and clapped his hands. Gray relaxed into his seat and Redding just smiled. This was a major victory, hard won to be sure.

"Get those pilots on board," Gray said. "And let's head back to our new allies. I think we've got some people to pick up and some loose ends to tie up before we get back home. Thank you everyone, for a job well done. I appreciate it more than you'll ever know."

As do we all, Olly said. *As do we all*.

Epilogue

Panther Five bailed out successfully and was found by one of the search and rescue shuttles. Leslie broke her leg but was otherwise unscathed. They brought her back to the Behemoth and admitted her to the sick bay where she was treated with a prognosis of a one hundred percent recovery.

Bear Four was no so lucky. They did eventually find debris from his escape pod but the majority of it was vaporized by the bombing run. Harlon Mitchel died a hero but that didn't comfort the rest of his wing. They mourned him when they got the news but Rudy took it the hardest. He promised to speak to the pilot's parents in person when they returned so they could hear first hand how bravely he faced his final few minutes.

Lieutenant Theresa Conway died of her wounds. Ensign Amos Roper survived and was locked in the brig once the medics stabilized his injury. He and Timothy Collins would be turned over to Earth military police upon arrival home and charged with treason. The evidence against them was damning but not nearly so bad as what they had on Admiral Jameson.

Gray intended to take that all the way to the top if necessary.

They connected again with Raeka from the Emancipated fleet after they combed the battlefield and assisted them with recovery of their own downed crew members. Gray sat in his chair, exhausted and ready for sleep but intent on tying up a few loose ends. He greeted the other commander with a smile.

"Hello again, Raeka. Glad we all made it."

"Our losses were heavy but not as bad as we've seen before," Raeka said. "I understand you had few casualties?"

"Some of those hits took lives," Gray replied, "but we came out fairly well. I hope you realize this isn't the last you've heard from those guys. They will be back eventually and you're going to need some help if you want to stand a chance. You can't fight amongst yourselves and hope to do battle with them too."

"We understand that," Raeka replied. "Our two governments will have a lot to chew on with the data we've collected. Will you stay and assist us?"

"I'm afraid we're not in any position to do that right now," Gray replied. "But we will certainly send help as soon as we return. The alliance has vessels specifically for this and now that we know you're out here, they'll make contact. You're not alone in this fight, I want you to understand that."

"We're honored by your willingness to sacrifice yourselves for us," Raeka said. "You could've left at any moment but chose to stay. That was unexpected...even after we fired on you."

"I couldn't let civilians suffer...not while we were combat effective." Gray stood from his seat. "We're preparing to go now, but you'll hear from us soon. I promise."

"Until we meet again, Captain Atwell." Raeka placed his hand over his chest and briefly bowed his head.

"Of course, Captain Anvinari." Gray saluted back in the traditional Earth way. "I look forward to a conversation under less...dire circumstances."

"As do I. Safe journeys, my friend."

Gray cut the com and turned to Adam. "You okay to take the con for now?"

"Yes, sir. I'm doing okay." Adam smirked. "I don't think I've ever seen you look so tired."

"I'm guessing that being the first person to try the shot the Doctor gave us probably didn't mean she had it right yet," Gray said. "I'm going to get some downtime. Let's get well away from the two fleets prior to jumping. Say...four hours out?"

"Sounds good, sir. I'm on it."

"Sir?" Clea stood up. "Do you mind if I walk with you back to your quarters?"

"Not at all, Clea. I wanted to talk to you anyway. Let's go."

They left, boarding the elevator. Neither spoke until it opened and even then they got a good ten feet before Clea finally broke the silence. "I would like to apologize for not relating the sabotage to you immediately. I was just distracted with everything else going on."

"It's fine," Gray replied. "I've already forgotten about it. Water under the bridge."

"I'm surprised about the traitors...about what they were willing to do."

Gray nodded. "Me too. But if Jameson's behind it, he can be persuasive with his hate fueled rhetoric. He'll go down for this. I'm only sorry they tried to use you as their scapegoat. I'm glad they failed to establish any real evidence. Doubt can be as bad as guilt to humans at times."

Clea nodded. "So I've seen. Thank you for standing by me. And trusting me to fix the shields."

"You were the only person who could do it." Gray paused. "I should check on Maury."

"Chief Engineer Higgins is asleep," Clea replied. "I tried to call down to speak to him but the doctor said he's been given a sedative to rest. They stabilized him and he'll be fine."

"What about that other crewman Conway shot?"

"They'll make it but it was touch and go for a time." Clea shrugged. "Apparently, she missed anything too vital...but it was close."

Gray shook his head. "Thank God."

"What do you think is going to happen when we get home?"

"We'll deliver our cargo, turn over our prisoners, testify on Jameson and wait for the next mission." Gray clapped her on the shoulder. "I don't think anything's changed in that regard."

"Good..." Clea smiled at him. "I'm not ready to go home yet."

"I wouldn't want to do this without you." Gray gestured to his quarters. "Now, if you don't mind, I'd like to get some sleep before we head back to Earth. See you later?"

"Count on it, sir." Clea offered him a salute. "Good night."

Printed in Great Britain
by Amazon